WORDS IN THE WIND

A BOOK OF SHORT STORIES

F. D. Brant

F. D. BRANT

F. D. Brant PO Box 522 Gresham Or 97030

Copyright © 2018 by F. D. Brant

All rights reserved. No part of this publication may be reproduced, distributed or transmitted in any form or by any means, without prior written permission.

F. D. Brant
PO Box 522
Gresham Or 97030
https://fdbrant.godaddysites.com/

Publisher's Note: This is a work of fiction. Names, characters, places, and incidents are a product of the author's imagination. Locales and public names are sometimes used for atmospheric purposes. Any resemblance to actual people, living or dead, or to businesses, companies, events, institutions, or locales is completely coincidental.

Book Layout © 2016 BookDesignTemplates.com

Words in the Wind/ F. D. Brant. -- 1st ed.
ISBN 978-1-946179-30-2

Books Written by F. D. Brant

Science Fiction Adventure

Of Gods Strangers and Messengers

Survival Trilogy

Time of Isolation

Desperate to Survive

A Taste of history Past

The Harsh Lands

Post-Apocalyptic

Unexpected Unplanned and into the Unknown

Discovery Trilogy

The Ones Before

Discovery

An Ancient Fire

Contemporary Christian Fiction

The Woman in the Snow

CONTENTS

Thoughts From the Author	1
The Soldier	3
Fire on the Mountain	11
A Week and a Day	38
The All Powerful	49
The Move	55
The Great Break	62
Holiday Short Stories	71
One Night Going Home	73
Breakdown	86
Dust	100
A Thanksgiving to Remember	120
Returning Home	126
A Christmas Story	137
A Darkness Incomplete	146
Storms	153
And it Came to Pass	172
Time Shared Time Lost	186
The Ornament	196
The Child	212

Thoughts From the Author

Welcome to my first novel of short stories. Many I wrote with the plan of submitting them to writing contests, and some were actually submitted. Others I wrote specifically for the blog, "Words in the Wind", which if you've noticed, is the title of this book. When I decided to put this together I wasn't quite sure of the format. What I mean here is, would I decide to order them by when I wrote them, or would be by subject or genre?

I thought about which would make a good opening short story, and if the order from there would simply progress so that there wouldn't be a huge shift. I also decided that I'd, like here, give an introduction to each story so that you as the reader would see where I was and what I saw when I wrote the story.

This book will be broken into two parts. The first is general short stories that might take place at any time or place during the year – because the stories aren't tied to any holiday or such. While the second half of the book is tied to holidays here in the USA – specifically Halloween, Thanksgiving, and Christmas. With the Thanksgiving and Christmas stories being Christian based.

If we were to look at the contest portion most submitted stories must meet specific criteria and if you fall outside of any of these requirements then your story is immediately disqualified. One the most important in this is usually word count. Normally these short story contests run the gambit of somewhere between one thousand five hundred to four thousand words. To understand how this would translate to a page count, according to the print book, you'd take the total words and divide it by either three hundred, or three hundred and fifty.

In many ways by having this specific limitation it forces the writer to clean up his or her writing. To get the full story and the impact desired inside that specific word count requires many rewrites. When one writes a novel then there is room to take the time to explain the situation. Short stories, not so much.

So normally I shift perspectives. In novels I write in third person. All my short stories are first person, bringing the world up close and personal. If you've picked this up to read please enjoy the many worlds, the personal stories told, and as the reader to be up close and personal to the protagonists that are presented here – F. D. Brant

The Soldier

Author's Notes

Anybody who followed my blog knows that I wrote a series of posts on gaming – computer gaming to be exact. And I have to admit to being "a gamer" since the nineties. This short story came about because of one of those games. For those who don't game then, as in all things, common phrases, and terminology would make no sense. Such things as collision, invisible walls, clipping, maps, and such all refer to the programing and game worlds.

If there are areas where you aren't supposed to go, within these worlds, then invisible walls are placed there, as well as changing the surface area making it impossible to maybe climb up a hill that normally would be easy. There are other ways to keep one within the playing field but these are the most common.

In this particular game world the walls weren't placed well and, as I call it, I "broke the map" and went outside the game world. I then explored this "off limits" area giving me insight into the playing field as well as how a game world is constructed. It was what I observed happening in this forbidden area that led to this story. And now you know . . . And for your reading pleasure, The Soldier.

The Soldier

I don't know when these doubts started entering my mind. This war seemed endless, with no definite victory or defeat – just one battle after another, or small skirmishes, or individual firefights followed by nothing but boredom. Soldiers would arrive and die and then were replaced. Where they even came from was unknown. As one would die the replacements would just appear and join our unit. There seemed to be an endless supply. What was going on, I mean really, what was happening here?

There had never been statements as to why this war or why we were fighting. We just fought with only the thoughts of surviving. I think I began to wonder when I realized that no one would ever speak of their past, of home, of loved ones, of the one they hoped to return to when the fighting ended. I started to think about this myself and realized that I could remember no past, only being here. No home . . . how can that be? I mean I am here, I am alive, and so I had to come from somewhere. Was I becoming crazy, and was I the only one that noticed these . . . irregularities?

Not only were we fighting an unknown enemy, but also there were wild dogs and such that would kill just as easily as an enemy bullet or knife. So attrition was not just from enemy fire. I think it was during one of those attacks from the wild dogs that the first doubts started entering my mind. There were four of us when the pack attacked, and while we were able to finally kill the pack they had taken down one of our team – one of our own. I bent down over the body to see if he was still alive and noticed to my surprise that the other two members of the team just walked off and continued their patrol. It was like they didn't even care . . . no that wasn't accurate . . . it was like once this one died he never existed and the two just continued on their patrol as if nothing happened.

Yes our comrade was dead, but why such a reaction from the rest of the squad? I was now far behind them, and yelled for them to wait. But either they ignored what I had yelled or never heard. They just continued their patrol as if it was all they were to do . . . as if nothing else mattered. So, rising from the body, I started following the remainder of the squad, although they were barely in sight. I could do nothing for our dead comrade other than report his loss when we got back to our base. But I suspected that somehow they were already aware of the loss and a new replacement would soon be there. How was this so? Again, was I imagining all of this, or truly was I going insane? Yet if I was asking myself these questions I felt that I could not be. Would someone who was insane ask himself or herself if they were? I think not, so I thought I then couldn't be crazy. But what was going on? I hurried to try and catch the squad, which seemed much too distant. I knew, most likely that if I caught them at all it would be at the end of our patrol. I suspected that I would hear about it from our officer when I got back. You know, "abandoning the squad over a dead member and not keeping up with the remainder of the squad to help keep them alive" . . . or something to that effect.

The route of our patrol took us through the fields among the oaks mixed with scattered pines, down a hill where there was a minor road. Once we reached the road we then would head back into our base, have a meal, and relax before repeating some other patrol. When I finally reached the road I saw that the squad was still well ahead of me and was not too far from entering back into the base. I tried to call out to them again, but again there was no response, just a continuation of the patrol. I looked around to make sure I was alone and when I looked back they were gone – disappeared, vanished like they never had been. I thought, no that couldn't be the way of it. They were not that far ahead and there was nothing where I last seen them that they could disappear behind. The road at this point was open; the surrounding lands were bare other than the grasses. There was no place to hide, no place to disappear like they just had. Where did they go? One cannot just disappear like that, yet . . . yet they did. I remember running down that road to the point where I thought they had disappeared, but in truth do not remember reaching it. The next memory I had was being back in camp, and the other two being there also, and yes there was a new soldier there, a replacement for the one we had lost on the patrol. How had they known so quickly? And why was there no reprimand from the officers about being separated from the squad? Had I imagined it all? All I could do was write this in my journal. It was comforting to me as it confirmed that I had not dreamed it. Or was the journal part of a dream?

I found myself second-guessing everything as to my sanity. Looking around to my comrades they just did not appear to have the worries or fears that I did. So I kept all this to myself. At this point I had nothing I could prove, and as such I knew that if I tried to explain what I felt, and had viewed, I would get a good laugh and be told that I had a great imagination. "After all, are we not at war? Were we not going to have casualties, were there not be replacements brought in to replace those losses?" Their questions were valid. It was just that how things were working just did not make any sense to me. Yet, the rest around me seemed to remain unconcerned.

Then something happened while out on one of those patrols – I cannot quite explain it. I guess it was something like an earthquake, well that is the best I can explain it. Again I had been a member of a squad of four, but the other three just disappeared right in front of me. I panicked so severely that I ran away from our assigned patrol area. I found myself completely outside of anything I was familiar with. I looked back at those solid buildings and I found that I was looking through them. *Looking through them*, how is this possible? I mean I had leaned against those walls and they supported me. Yet I swore that from here they were invisible with the roofs floating in the air. At first it shook me to my core. But when the world and my life did not end, I calmed down and then curious started walking around this new area. It seemed to be vacant, and yet the grass and trees were here. The weather continued with the wind blowing and the clouds scooting across the sky. Yet from here while all of this was real, the buildings continued to go from visible to invisible all according to my perspective and position.

I decided that since there appeared to be no danger, and I had travel rations that I would continue to search out this new area. After all, the officers would probably like to know about this. But would they in the end believe it? If one was not here, and as far as I knew I was the only one, then how could it be proven? I did not even know if there was a way to get back. I did not know how it happened in the first place. Somehow I had to find proof. I had no camera, and any description that I might give would be laughed off as some joke. I searched desperately around for anything that would prove what I had seen here. There was nothing, just nothing. I was becoming desperate. Was I the only one who had come across this? No there would have to have been others. I needed to believe that.

I wasn't due back to base for a while so I decided to continue to explore this unknown area continuing to walk away from the base area deeper into the fields. Off in the distance something did not look right. I mean off in the distance something really did not look right! I ran towards it to find out what it might be, and had to stop quickly. Breathing hard from the running and having chills run up and down my spine I stood on the edge of a cliff. Did I say cliff . . . no, cliff was inaccurate; I stood on the edge of an abyss. It was as if the lands just ended here. In the distance I saw the blue sky and white clouds. But at the edge looking straight across and down all was just gray. Not gray like when a fog is covering the land, but gray like there was nothing there.

After catching my breath I started following this edge around to see if anything changed. Where I was I climbed hills walked down into small valleys but the gray never changed over that edge. Eventually I reached a road and like the land the road just ended at the edge, as if it was cut off. I saw wild dogs running up and down the road chasing wild boars. For them all was normal, but for me nothing would be normal ever again.

Then I noticed someone approaching, and to my surprise it was the general. Standing at attention when he arrived, he waved me off."

The general then said, "Now you know."

"Sir . . . know what? What I am seeing here . . . I don't understand."

"Believe me it is something that is very difficult to understand, but I will try and explain. And oh by the way, when you return back to camp, and you will, you will be an officer."

"An officer? Why? I've always been enlisted."

"True, but once this has been discovered then it is automatic." Then waving me off he continued, "You see we have been watching you. And believe it or not every officer has discovered what you have. They, including myself, were enlisted also." Then sighing he said, "How do I say this? This world, the world that we live in is not real. We are not real. That is why none of us seems to have any history other than the base. That is why when one of us dies that he is immediately replaced. That is why there are no families or loved ones. This is a game world created by someone, and we live and die here. But since we are not real we cannot really die. I think that when we cease to exist as this person that we come back as another. This is what is called a map, and as you can see, it has an end, and you are now standing there. I have to assume that there are other such maps but we will always be here at the calling of this game world and there is nothing we can do about it, nothing at all . . ."

Silent, I followed the general back to base in shock. These answers weren't what I expected at all. We then crossed some kind of threshold and I looked at myself, indeed I was an officer as he had foretold, and now a leader of men who were safe in their ignorance, as I wish I was

Fire on the Mountain

Author's Notes

If any out there have lived through a natural disaster, then you can personally relate to this story. One might ask, "How is it that you can be so sure in your descriptions?" And the simple answer is while this is a fictitious short story, much of what stated here is fact and personal. Simply stated I and my family lived through what is presented here.

In fact the region where this takes place, and while I write this, wildfires are presently burning. It has been a winter where there has been little rain. So little in fact that deserts have received more moisture, leaving the backcountry tender dry and ready to burn. Personally I know a bit about wildland firefighting as it was my occupation in my youth.

So unlike most of my short stories I had no need to create imagery in my mind's eye. I witnessed, and experienced it personally. And those images from that time will remain with me. Not that experiences from my time as a firefighter will fade with time, because they won't.

Something to take away from this: We believed that we'd be able to protect our homes, and while our lead time was short by having this attitude there were items left that might have been saved. Have a family plan in place, and be sure that everybody knows and understands that plan. Make sure important items are where you can reach them quickly and are not spread out. In the end you may only have minutes to evacuate. Understand that in the chaos communication is critical. So if you face a natural disaster, plan for the worst, and hope for the best.

Fire on the Mountain

The devastation was complete. Not a building or home was left standing. As he stood there with his wife and children all he could do was shake his head. There had been more than adequate clearing around the buildings to keep them from burning. But here was the proof that what they had tried to accomplish wasn't enough. "Total loss," he said to no one in particular – not that it wasn't obvious. "Maybe we can find something that survived . . . but looking, I think that the heat from this fire probably gives us little chance of finding anything at all."

Not sure as to what to do, he signaled them to just spread out and check everything. Years of work and effort gone in a few minutes as if it never had been. While the house wasn't anything special, in fact, it was too small for their family, it still had been home. They were not rich people, if the truth were told; they barely made lower middle class. They were living on family property in the country and there had been three homes here, and all three were gone. Of course they were not the only ones. All the homes on the mountain had been destroyed.

It was now Tuesday, and even though the fire had passed through this area on Sunday the skies were still filled with smoke and ash. They had a cargo container they had used for storage and at this time, whatever was inside was burning. With no way to put the fire out all they could do was watch helplessly as the flames consumed what little they had left. The fire had destroyed the water storage tank and many of the feed lines, so there was no water available to fight the fire . . . and no electricity.

Coming back that morning as they traveled the dirt road home they saw the mountain bare of greenery with only black and gray ash, with the skeletons of the chamise, scrub oak, and manzanita standing and pointing to the sky. The power poles were all down, with many lying in the road, all showing heavy fire damage. The lines themselves lay everywhere and in many places they had to detour around them. As even at this moment, while it appeared that there was no way for power to be in them, they could not be sure. With no tension on the lines, they lay on the ground, black against the lighter soils, appearing to more like snakes than something that just a short time ago allowed them to have electricity.

As they had driven in that Tuesday, it had appeared that they had entered a war zone. One of the first things they noticed, as they had stopped and stood outside of their car, was the quiet. The only thing heard was the wind. From this vantage point they saw much of the surrounding countryside and nowhere could they find a place where the fire hadn't been. The smells, in the air, were very strong of burned chaparral and wood. The world they were seeing was foreign to them. Without the vegetation to cover the mountain it was now a stranger. Everything was laid bare. Never had they seen so many rocks and boulders. Everywhere they looked they saw small dust devils forming, running a short distance, disappearing, and then new ones picking up the dance. After a brief time, they continued on into where their home had been, along with two other homes belonging to other family members.

WORDS IN THE WIND

What did one do after something like this happens? They, like many in the backcountry, had no insurance. With the locations being so remote, there were few companies that would insure, and if they would, the costs would be so high that it easily could be more expensive than a regular monthly mortgage payment. Few could afford such a thing. So one took their chances, and this time those chances had gone against them. Looking across to the other two destroyed homes, they watched as the other family members were doing much the same thing as they were, looking at the destruction and trying to find something that may have survived. He knew that they were in just about the same shape from their body language that even from a distance was so easy to read. Again, where were all of them going to go from here?

None of them had ever been in this situation. They had become refugees in their own land, with no place to stay, no food, and no water. The only advantage was the country where it had happened. Had it been a third world country then there would be no immediate help, but here at least there would be, and close to immediate. Still, they planned on staying here, but needed to at least come up with some type of shelter, and get a generator, so that with some repairs, they could get water flowing again. "Standing around isn't getting any of this done. Allie, I'm going over and talk with the other family members. You can either join me or stay here with the boys and see what you can find."

"I think I'll stay for now. Let me know what you find out and what you all decide, okay?"

"Of course, just have the boys take a bunch of pictures. We may need them later, and I guess just be careful. I should be back shortly, since I need to know how the rest want to deal with this."

As he left he turned around and looked back at his wife, who in an unguarded moment, had let down. He could see from the slump of her shoulders that she felt completely defeated, at loss as to what to do, and where to go. She had turned in that moment and saw him looking back at her. She responded with a smile . . . a sad smile, but at least he could tell she was trying. His heart went out to her and he knew that he must continue to be strong for all of them. As it would be so easy to become negative and allow this to completely take over their lives.

* * *

It was Saturday late in October, and so far the rains hadn't come. Fourth year of drought, and all the surrounding chaparral was dormant, and extremely dry. If a fire started then the chamise and chaparral would act like flash fuels – with the oils in the chamise and the low humidities it would burn hot and fast. The chaparral around their area hadn't burned in over 50 years, and as such, was prime burning material. In some areas it stood over twelve feet high and was so thick one could not crawl through it let alone walk. In almost every area there was much that was dead, leaving the whole area a tinderbox just waiting for the *right* moment. Yet they felt somewhat safe with the clearing they had.

That *right* moment began that Saturday afternoon, when off to the north he saw the beginnings of a convection column of smoke. He immediately went back inside and turned on their scanner to monitor the fire situation. Unfortunately, very little was received, as most of the fire traffic was hitting a different repeater, and it wasn't one they could get, simply because of the mountains between themselves and that repeater. Commercial radio and TV was worthless as they covered some of the large bedroom communities and ignored the backcountry. The only confirmation they had was the building smoke column, and it was building rapidly. All he could hope was that it would stay north of them and not be a threat.

Add to this the threat of Santa Ana winds coming in; it looked like a disaster waiting to happen. They needed to get that fire out, and out now. Once the winds hit it, it would be over, and there would be an extremely large wildland fire out of control with no chance of it stopping until the strong winds quit. Those winds were hot dry winds out of the east, northeast, and southeast. Speeds could be up to 100 miles per hour, and humidities could drop into the single digits, creating explosive situations, and many times, firestorms. He had seen whole canyons go up at once – scary, but beautiful all at the same time. It had been said that in the heavy areas of this chaparral that if one acre all burned at once that the energy created from that one acre would be equal the energy created by the bomb dropped on Hiroshima or Nagasaki at the end of WWII.

***

Back when he had been a wildland firefighter, he had been in one blowup situation, and it had been pushed by these winds. With other fire trucks they were making a stand along one of the many dirt roads through the forest. If they could hold it here at this point then they probably could keep it out of some of the more populated areas that this one seemed to be heading towards. They had anchored themselves to a burned area caused by a spot fire earlier that day that they had extinguished. Off to the west of them was a ranger station and in the opposite direction was their escape route. The truck was faced towards the closest blacktop road, while a few miles away were initially out of the danger zone, and the primary escape route. The secondary escape route would be back to that ranger station.

All through that afternoon and into early evening they awaited the main fire. Then, when it arrived it did so with a vengeance. As it had earlier in the day the fire ignited numerous spot fires across that dirt road and their line, but this time they were having difficulty in extinguishing the large number of small fires that was igniting. Then the main fire ran down the hill, pushed by those winds and reached them. Suddenly there was just too much fire for them to handle. The spot fires began to combine and became a second front. Now stuck between the main fire, and the spot fire created second front, they knew they had to abandon their defensive position. Word had reached them that the fire had jumped the road in the direction of their planned escape and now that direction was no longer a safe option.

At this point no artificial light was needed, as the whole area around them was fully engulfed in flame. Yet, they had to turn the fire truck around – a real difficulty on this one lane dirt road –

and then get out of there. He was sent out to help

direct the driver on safe backing and jockeying of the fire truck so that they would be able to go back towards the ranger station. While out there doing that job he noticed that everything that could burn was burning, so with care and speed they successfully got the truck turned around. Then the driver had everyone climb into the cab and he drove rapidly out of the area. As he did, they had fire lapping over the truck. Had any of them remained outside, in the crew area, most likely, they would have been burned.

* * *

Now here on this Saturday, these many years later, it became obvious that there was a great possibility that they would be facing the same situation here. Because of the years of living here, and his experience, he felt that they had adequate clearance around everything. To the west and northwest they were clear to bare earth at about 150 yards. The remaining directions of the compass it was no less than 150 feet. The other homes on the property were similarly protected. With the tank full at 2200 gallons of water, and hand tools for firefighting he felt their chances of surviving a fire was very good. So, for the rest of Saturday, they watched nervously as the smoke column continued to build. Then as night approached the predicted Santa Ana winds arrived. But with darkness they were no longer able to see the smoke column, and because of the mountains between them could not see the glow from the actual fire.

Again, they continued try to get as much information as possible. Every once in a while something would come over the scanner talking about moving equipment up, and then they would switch to the other repeater and nothing else would be heard. There was nothing helpful from the commercial side, as once again, they ignored the backcountry, as if it didn't exist. He was without vital information and hadn't received enough even to know what the situation was, other than the winds had picked up, and the fire and was being pushed towards the coast. So they remained up that night until midnight when one of their sons came home from work. They asked him if he had anything new to add, and he actually knew less than they did. So exhausted from the day they went to bed.

Two hours later the phone rang. The son picked up and then knocked on the bedroom door saying that it was Heather. Groggy, Allie picked up the phone, listened and then turned to him and said, "Heather says they are leaving, the fire is at their door right now!"

"That can't be, as it was still a long ways away from them, when we went to bed," he responded. Turning around and looking at the clock he continued, "Oh my, that was only two hours ago! Hold on, I'll go outside and look, I can at least check, and see." He got out of bed, put his clothes on and said to himself quietly, "Guess not much sleep tonight." Then headed outside and quickly stopped and was shocked by what he saw. He immediately turned back and let everyone know that as far as he could see all he saw was fire. The front was miles long, stretching from the north at the furthest point that was visible, all the way to the west, down into Lakestown, where the daughter lived. How was that possible? Never in his life had he seen a fire move this fast. There would be no sleep for any of them this night. Now for sure it would have to be monitored. If the wind direction changed, it would be a real threat to them.

After that one phone call from Heather, there was no further contact, and so they had no idea what had happened from that point on. Were they able to get out safely, and if so, where were they? Much later they learned that she and her boyfriend barely got out with the clothes on their backs, before the fire was on them. Shortly after they had left, the raging fire consumed the house they were living in. (It was days before that contact would be made, from that initial phone call, and they would know that she was safe.)

Standing outside in the night air with the winds at his back, he watched as the fire made runs up the mountain to the west of them. It did appear that the whole world was on fire. The only thought at this time came unbidden. The winds were at his back, giving them a good chance of, maybe, being missed. But in his mind, he had real doubt. If the fire had moved this fast, and was consuming everything in sight, what was to prevent it from coming their way? At about this time, Allie came out and handed him a cup of coffee. She nervously watched the fire and said, "What's your feeling on this? I've never seen anything like this, and really don't want to see anything like this again, to be truthful."

Putting his arm around her waist he replied, "If, from my experience, I based this on the fire behavior with these winds involved, I would suspect that we would be out of danger. But I have a gut feeling that this time it will reach us."

She shuddered a little, while looking at the running fire and asked, "Are you sure? This scares me. Again I have never seen so much fire in my life."

"No . . . no I'm not sure, but there is something about this one that is telling me that we will be facing it soon enough. I just hope that we can protect the houses – our homes. I know that we have many advantages set up here. The fire has to run downhill to get to us from any direction but to the southeast, and most of the area is somewhat flat – plus add in the clearing that has been done . . . well, if it is a normal fire or even a normal Santa Ana pushed fire we'd have a chance . . ." Then trailing off he said, ". . . a small one but, a chance."

She stayed out with him for a few more minutes saying nothing, then turned around and went back inside. He could understand her feelings and fears. Heck he had them too, and he was an experienced wildland firefighter. He took a flashlight and walked around their home to confirm everything that could be done had been. He then looked over at the other two houses on the property, seeing their porch lights on looking quite alone in the darkness . . . two isolated ships in a sea of blackness. He then noticed someone approaching him from his brother's home. In a short time he saw that it was his brother. "What do you think?" Mike asked as he came into hearing range.

"It's a worrisome thing . . . a very worrisome thing. I've never seen anything move this fast, period."

"Do you think we are in trouble?"

Shaking his head he said, "Yeah, very big trouble. I would have thought the work we all have done around here would be enough. Now, with this thing, I'm not sure at all. All we can hope for is that I'm wrong and it will either miss us or what we've done is enough. I think if it does come, we will try and make a stand, but, at the same time, I think we need to be prepared to leave. As you well know, there is only one way in and one way out of here. So if that is blocked by the fire we could really be in for some very serious trouble."

"Okay, I'll head back and let the family know. Have you gone down and spoken to mom yet?"

"No, not yet – figured I would do that in the morning. She has her hands full with dad's condition and needs all the sleep she can get. I think we have at least that much time, and there isn't much she can do anyway."

Laughing a nervous laugh, Mike said, "Its morning now. I think somewhere around 3:30 or 4:00 A.M. But I know what you mean, daylight. Okay, I'll see you again after daylight, and we can, as a family, plan our strategies."

* * *

With the rising of the sun and no one in their household getting any more than 2 hours sleep, he headed back out to observe. As it had been all of Saturday, it continued with little hard information. Other than what they saw visually, there was nothing presented that was useful to them. It was frustrating to not have any vital information. It made it impossible to plan, or to know what really was happening. So he waited until he saw movement down at his parent's home before leaving to go visit and find out how they were handling it all. Looking at the area where the fire was burning, all he saw was smoke. With the light of day the all too visible smoke column had replaced the glow of the fire and the runs it had made. It was huge, period. It ran from the southwest to the north where there was a strong break between the dark black-gray smoke, and the clear blue sky. It was as if someone had drawn a dividing line, telling the smoke that it could not cross here. Looking at that smoke he saw that it was boiling up hot and heavy rising quickly to the heavens. This was a hot fire.

He eventually reached the house and found his mother standing there on the porch watching the same thing he had been watching, as he approached the house. Shaking his head he asked, "Spectacular isn't it? How are you holding up here? I know with dad in the shape he's in that you have this all to do on your own. If you need any assistance please let us know, and I'll send the boys down to help. Oh later, not that you cannot see it here, come up with us, as we're on a little higher ground and you can, at least, see further to the west."

"So far everything's fine . . . and spectacular doesn't adequately describe it at all. This one's a monster. I think from what I can remember that this is even worse than the one that came through to the south of us about thirty years ago. Yes I know, you weren't here for that one. You were in the army at the time." She paused a moment and shrugged, "So far dad's not a problem, but I'll take you up on having your boys down here to help if that's okay."

"Yup, that's okay. I think, a little later, I'm going to take the road further in, and see if I can spot what this thing is going to do. I'll take a handi-talkie with me so that I can keep everyone informed. I think initially, we will try and protect the homes here. But, I think that we will have to be prepared to leave, just in case we cannot do that. Won't know what we will be able to do or not until the fire actually approaches, if it does."

"You think it will?"

"Again, not sure, but I do have a feeling that this one will not miss us as the others have in the past. I sure wish I knew more but the scanner is quiet, and the radio and TV is worthless."

"Very true, all they keep covering is some of the rich bedroom communities. It's like we don't exist at all."

"Stupid isn't it. Anyway, I'll head back up. All we can do is what we are doing right now . . . Probably will see you sometime later." With that he headed back up the hill to their house and continued to watch and worry. All that could be seen by any of them was the smoke, and it was dark, black, angry and rising rapidly. Changing colors from white to black as it just continued to boil into the sky. Again because of where they were the base of this smoke wasn't visible and because of that there was no way to make an intelligent decision as to what they should to do.

He remembered that he needed to call his boss at home since it was obvious to him that there would be no way he would be at work on Monday. Plus he needed to contact his replacement to let her know that she probably would be working the office for at least a few days, how long . . . he really had no idea. Turning to Allie he then said, "I think we need to both call our respective supervisors and let them know what we are facing here, and let them know that we probably will not be in tomorrow at all. Have you heard from our daughter yet?"

"That's a good idea. I'll go ahead and call Sue and let her know our situation, and no, not a word. Frankly I'm worried, but there is nothing either you or I can do. We don't even know where they went when they left last night."

"Yeah, once again without any facts or anything that will help we are completely blind here, and that is a real problem. You know I think we had better load up our cars with something. And yes I know, if it misses us then we will have to put it back. But what if it doesn't? Then we would be kicking ourselves for not doing it. I think I am going to head up on the road where it is higher and see if I can see anything. Keep the handi-talkie on and I'll let you know what I see. Keep your ear to the scanner as maybe something that will help might finally come over it, and once you have gotten what you feel we need then send the boys down and help mom as she's alone with dad."

Nervously Allie looking around replied, "Okay, but what is your plan? You are the one with the experience here and I for one am quite nervous about this whole thing."

"Yeah, I know. So am I, since I have nothing to go on other than the smoke. I'm hoping that we can stay here and protect the houses. But much depends on what the fire does once it gets here. And until it does, I truthfully will have no idea. If it approaches us like a normal . . . even a Santa Ana pushed fire then we should have a chance of keeping it away from the houses. I think that it will be approaching us from the west. And if it is doing that it will be burning into the wind making the fire fight for every inch and slowing it down. Add to it that it must burn downhill to reach us, which again should slow it down, all of this giving us further chances for protecting things. Later I'm going to call a meeting and kind of go over everything with everyone. But in the end it may turn out that we have no choice and have to run. Once I finish my call to my boss then I will go out and see what I can see. I just hope I can see something that will help us."

He then started walking around trying to find a signal for the cell phone so he could make the call to his boss. The signal strength here was so variable that from one moment to the next it would drift enough to drop the signal. It was something he never understood as their location was completely open from the south to the northwest. Nothing at all blocking any approaching signal, but it was always weak. Finally finding a point where it appeared that it would be strong enough to make the call he called his boss and informed him of the situation. The boss asked to be kept informed of what was happening. He then called his replacement and alerted her that she would have the office for a while, again how long he didn't know.

Once the calls were completed he waved at Allie and headed out in the car to see what he could learn. He stopped briefly at his parent's house to see how things were going and to again let her know that once they were finished up there that his boys would be down here to help her with anything she needed help with . . . And also that the plan was to try and protect if the fire did get there. Then with the binoculars and handi-talkie he drove further in on the dirt road to both put him higher than where they were located and a little closer to the approaching fire.

Further in on this road were five other families and their homes. He wanted to head past two of those homes and get closer to one of the others as from there he could partially look down into the canyon to the west where he figured the fire would approach. As he continued in that direction he ran into one of the families. Stopping briefly he exchanged greetings and found that they were at loss as to what to do. He understood this, as this was to be their first such fire and if you hadn't lived with them you just wouldn't know. He gave them whatever suggestions he could and then moved further in saying that if the fire was coming that he would warn them to give them time to get out.

From where he parked he looked down on the family property and saw people moving around. Unfortunately he had a better view of the property than the canyon where he suspected the fire would come out of – if it did. There was a single hill to the northwest that sat by itself and the smoke was boiling hot, black, and heavy off the west side. The rest of the smoke appeared to be further to the west. It was just hard to say what was going to happen at this point. Calling back to Allie on the handi-talkie he said, "This really doesn't look good, but so far there is nothing on our side. I'm going to come back briefly so that we can load my car up, grab something to eat, and then return here. If I see it come out of the canyon it will be from this location that I will be able to see it. Plus according to how it comes out will let me know what we are facing. See you shortly."

He punished the car heading back, but it was becoming more obvious to him that they were not going to get missed. There was no definite proof yet, but enough evidence to conclude that sometime that day they would be trying to protect what they owned. When he entered the property he stopped briefly at each house and passed on what he saw and then headed up to his home and got out and explained to the boys that it wasn't looking very good. *And still the winds blew strongly out of the east.* That smoke told him that it was still a very hot and rapid spreading fire. And the shock was that it appeared to be burning into the wind like it was being pushed by the wind. It should not be that way but it seemed that this fire was ignoring such things. Leaving him to conclude that most likely this fire was fuel and topography driven, and that scared him.

He called a brief meeting with the 3 families and explained where they should meet and that according to what the fire was doing when it came in would then determine what they would do if anything. "Okay, shortly I will be returning up to where I was so that I can monitor the fire. I will continue to keep in contact, but understand that if it does come up this side that once I call it in then we probably will only have thirty minutes or less before it will be on us. I sure do hope we can protect our homes. By the way has anyone seen any fire trucks or equipment anywhere?"

No one had and that was a worrisome thing. Why with thirteen homes back in the area, was there no one around? He thought that if they had one truck that they would easily defend the homes, but with just their hoses and a gravity fed water system it would be so much more difficult. He knew most of the people who lived back on the mountain and most would try and save what they had. But where was the protection they paid for? It was strangely absent. While he knew that with the size of this fire that the fire fighters would be thinly spread, there should be at least someone coming around to inform them of what was happening. Possibly the Forest Service, maybe the Sheriff's Department, or even the Highway Patrol. But to have no one made him feel much too isolated. All the phone lines where tied up or down, and the cell system was now overwhelmed and useless – leaving him frustrated, and a little fearful. What was going on here?

It was entering early afternoon and it was time to head back up and see what was happening. So he got back into his car and drove back out to the overlook where he had monitored the fire earlier that day. Much seemed the same even though a couple of hours had passed since he was last here. Yet studying the smoke he saw a heavy black and gray column that now appeared to be much closer. He suspected that the fire had finally crossed the canyon and was on their side. Studying the terrain in front of him he determined a couple of scenarios. One of the two would have a better outcome for them.

These scenarios were based on his experience. He felt that by looking at the terrain that according to where the fire came out the canyon would be either good or bad for them. So he waited and monitored and talked with the neighbors as they passed him. From the neighbors further in, none had actually seen any flames as of yet, but had come to the same conclusion he had. It would only be a matter of time before the fire would be upon them, and where was the fire department? He almost wished that the fire would get here and almost immediately felt guilty by such feelings. But he knew the reason why. Once it showed itself then finally there would be something concrete instead of this unknown.

He continued to watch the one smoke column and he knew that as the fire neared the top of the canyon and revealed itself that it would first show in the smoke. Because the heat from the fire affected the smoke it would start moving much faster and of course the further from the source the slower the smoke would rise. He continued to watch and saw that it was starting to pick up rapidly, and now he knew for sure it was about to crest on their side of the canyon. Almost holding his breath he watched, never taking his eyes off the smoke. Then the fire crested the top of the canyon and was now on top and heading east towards their homes. And in the scenarios he had created in his mind this point and direction was the worst. Slumping his shoulders he knew they were in serious trouble, but still hoped that they could protect the small ranch.

He stayed a few more minutes just to confirm what his eyes had shown him, and then called back to the ranch warning them that it was on the way and be prepared. As he drove back he saw one of the new neighbors sitting in their truck watching. He stopped and warned them it was here and it was time to either protect or evacuate, there would no other choices available. He then got back to the ranch and prepared as best they could to defend. Above them on another piece of property sat a two-story home on a twenty acre parcel. He watched the family moving around the house. They were well cleared also. But again this fire just seemed unusual. Thirty years earlier a fire had burned through this county and at the time was the biggest in not only this county's history, but in the recorded state history. Yet, this one seemed to be burning faster, hotter, and probably in the end would be much larger than that previous fire.

Once again he went over what everyone was supposed to do, and then with one final meeting at the safety area all went to their individual homes to do what they could. Now all they could do was wait, hope, and pray that they would be spared. They didn't have long to wait as the first signs of the approaching fire showed itself. Then a wall of flame of unbelievable height showed itself as it started running downhill. The flames were twice the height of that 2-story home! Looking at the inadequate equipment they had to defend their homes he knew right then and there it was a lost cause. If the fire was that intense burning against the wind and running downhill there was no chance. Oh to have a fire truck right now, but they did not, so could not do anything but leave, to abandon all they had, and hope that what had been done earlier would be enough. But in his heart he knew that if no one was here to put out the small fires that would start that there truly no chance of anything surviving.

Going back to the safety area and meeting area he let all know that there would be no chance and they would have to leave. Not only had he seen that the front was approaching from the northwest, but saw a second front approaching from directly west. One front would have been hard, but two impossible. Again admitting defeat he told all that there was nothing they could do other than leave. So from being on the defense to leaving, all grabbed what they could and began the drive out of the property. It was now around three in the afternoon. So approximately twelve hours after receiving the call from their daughter about the fire being at her door, it was now at theirs.

Their youngest son who was fifteen at the time had never really driven anything, but now had no choice. They only had one automatic and he was given this one to drive, a small pickup with a camper shell on its bed. None of the other 3 cars were large so overall even with the pickup not much could be taken. Before leaving he took one more walk through their home wondering if this would be the last time he would ever do this. He closed doors and checked windows to try and make it as safe as possible and then finally left and closed the front door, heading over to his car and then took one last look and began the drive out. He stopped briefly at his mother's house and told her that there was nothing they could do and all would have to evacuate. He waited until she got dad into their truck and started their drive out. He noticed that she had very little in the back of her truck.

What had happened? He had sent to boys down to help her put some stuff away just in case they had to leave, but he saw that very little was there. When the boys had returned from their assistance of their grandmother they had mentioned nothing so he assumed that everything that needed to be done had been. But now it was quite obvious that nothing had. He thought that maybe if he stopped and got out of his car that he could save something for them but immediately realized that there would be no time. All that time was now gone and it was either leave now or face the chance of not getting out at all. Shaking his head the only thought he had at the moment was that once again with no information being passed on, it left him ending with the wrong conclusion. And now all that his parents had collected for all their lives would be gone and there would be nothing he could do to change that now.

He remembered the end tables that his dad had brought back from Japan when he was there during the Korean conflict, and the beautiful dragon dishes, and so many other irreplaceable things that made their house their own. Now taking a last look he got back in his car and reluctantly drove out of the yard knowing in his heart that this would be the last time he would see any of this. They had been here for forty seven years, and now just had to abandon it all. *Where was the protection they had paid for?* Why hadn't there been anyone at all to come out and inform them of what was coming? Just nothing, nothing at all . . .

Eventually he caught up with the other vehicles and they stopped briefly at a point that overlooked the property and from there they saw the fire raging and starting to cross the west field with a vengeance. They had barely beaten the front out. Now another factor had entered in showing him that had they stayed they really would have been in trouble. Instead of just two points where the fire was approaching there actually was three. Unknown to them while they were still there a third front was approaching from the canyon and would have trapped them between the visible front coming from the west and this one that would have come in from the east. Defeated, all that they tried to do had failed. They then continued the drive out on the dirt road, onto the blacktop, and entered the town that their address was attached to and immediately ran into a gridlocked road as everyone in the area was attempting to evacuate the area. The roads had never been built to handle such traffic, and it simply became a large parking lot.

Now there was a new danger. With so much traffic and little movement if the fire came through this area there would be much injury and death. No one would be able to outrun this fire on foot, and it was obvious at this moment that no one would be able to drive out. A second problem then developed as they became separated. Fortunately with the handi-talkies they stayed in communication and at the bottom of the hill there was a small parking lot where they got back together. Now it was only his immediate family as his brother with his family and his parents were nowhere to be found. Once back on the road they were directed to an evacuation center which was a parking lot of a small shopping center to the east of the fire. They remained here until around 2 A.M., when another evacuation order was given as the same fire was threatening the shopping center.

Information was sparse and they were sent west to go to either a high school or a stadium. In the process of making this trek, they became separated due to poor directions of the ones in charge. Again thanks to the handi-talkies there were able to keep in contact and decided to go to the high school where they would meet up again. On the trip down to the high school they passed many areas that were engulfed in flames. They saw a number of houses fully involved and it seemed that the whole area, as far as they could see, was somehow burning. Eventually reaching the high school they spent the rest of Sunday, and then Monday there not getting much sleep at all. In fact by the time Tuesday arrived they had just about four hours sleep since Saturday night.

Then on Tuesday they returned and found all was gone. They then heard the story of what had happened with the rest of the family and how they had been back on the property late Sunday night after the fire had come through and destroyed everything. Even still there had been some small miracles as there had been birds in pens there, and they had survived, while everything around them was nothing but devastation. The other miracle was that no one in the family had been hurt or killed, while others had perished in the fire.

* * *

When it was all over this fire had burned faster, hotter, and had covered more acreage than the last largest fire in this county's history, and in the end becoming almost twice the size of the other. Many questions were raised afterwards, as there seemed to have been some major incompetence in the handling of the fire. Forecasts had shown that the winds would be arriving and if any wild fire did start suppression would have to be immediate before the Santa Ana winds had an opportunity to spread the fire. Such a fire did start and the ones in charge refused to allow any to suppress the fire. The result from this inaction was unleashing of the largest fire, not only is this county's history, but once again in the state.

A Week and a Day

I   Author's Notes

Imagery plays a big part in my novels, and short stories, and this one is no different. I saw a home sitting in a rural setting surrounded by trees. The home was two stories with a separate two-story garage. The second story of the garage might be considered an apartment or workshop or whatever the owners wanted it to be. There was a covered walkway between the two buildings connecting that apartment space with the main home making it easy to move between the two.

In the front of the home was a dirt driveway which was covered in snow. From there towards the north since the home had a north-south orientation the lands rose slightly before disappearing into the trees beyond. The home was warm and inviting, with the exterior being partially of log construction. Time of year would be around the Christmas holidays, and no, this isn't one of my Christmas annual stories.

With what I've been seeing with the country where I live I saw one of the directions that we were heading, and it wasn't a direction I wanted to see us go. So with those thoughts I extended this out to sometime deep in the future where the nation went from being an open and free country to one that had closed its borders, suppressed their citizens, and took whatever they – the government or state – wanted. There was nothing citizens could do to prevent it.

In a sense the story becomes a warning of where we might go if we do not remain diligent. And the story, as is most of my short stories, is told in first person. In this case the story is seen through the eyes of an individual who watches the border and is from the country that borders this one.

A Week and a Day

We'd received word that there was a family that was looking for asylum in our country. The family was just an ordinary family with no special talents or skills that would have been required in the past. The nation where they were presently living had begun to tighten their borders, and to put greater pressure on the citizens within those borders, to "toe the party line" so to speak, and any who did not were punished. So it was with this knowledge that the change of policy had come down through the channels that any who wanted to be free from there would be given the opportunity through our underground. From there the assignment came to my department to see if such a thing would be possible. When we researched what we knew, there were many favorable factors that said that we could pull this off, and even though our window would be small – no more than a week, plus a day or two – we felt it was doable.

Since this area where this family lives was an area that I had hunted when I was young and before the shutdown of the borders, I was the one who would lead the team on the ground – very unusual I know, especially since I had been out of the field end of this work for quite a few years – age has a way of doing that. But because of the small window that we had to work with my experience and knowledge were critical. Especially if we were to be successful and defeat the repressive government that now controlled that country. And we wanted to frustrate that government and pull their victims out of their hands at every opportunity. It made me smile every time we'd been successful in the past. Of course it was common for entire families to disappear under the present government and no one the wiser as to what had happened to them. But we on the outside were quite aware of what transpired and it was ugly.

The borders were patrolled regularly plus they had electronic surveillance making it difficult to pass over those borders. Still, if one knew where to look, there were always weaknesses in any system and this one was no different. With it late in the year, and it being winter, close to the time of the annual celebration that was now called, "The Winter Solstice Celebration", instead of what it had always been known before, we went to work. So with the team organized we headed for the border in a snowstorm figuring that this would at least keep the patrols down to a minimum. No one in their right mind wanted to be out in this stuff. After all, with the strength of the winds, the falling and blowing snow, the freezing temperatures, one might easily die, and it was so much nicer to remain by a warm cheery fire. The terrain also favored us and created large holes in their electronic network. Of course their goal was more to keep their citizens inside their borders than keep others out. So like the old USSR, not much was truly known about what was happening inside the borders other than what could be transmitted or smuggled out.

Who really knew what had happened to bring this family under suspicion of this government, but we suspected that some official decided that he liked the property that was owned by this family and to get it simply meant that he had to eliminate the family and then claim it for the state, for which, of course, he would manage. Again, from many of the conversations that we had, from the ones who had escaped, we knew that this was a common practice. After all who could stop the Secret Police, or the corruption and control, which existed there? It was our job to be like the hyenas that worry the lion after a kill so that we could get our share. Every time we were successful in rescuing any from their grasp was a win for us. Of course we were unable to be successful each and every time. It would be nice, but that is not reality, and yes, if we wanted to be completely honest we had failed a number of times. But each success meant that we would show the world that they were not invincible, and we would be sure that the facts would be transmitted back into those closed borders to give the suppressed citizens hope that someday this would end or that they would have their chance to leave.

With these thoughts we parked our vehicles, hidden deep in one of the many valleys, and headed, on foot, to a point well known to us. It was rarely patrolled and the electronic surveillance had so many holes that it could have been Swiss cheese. Still, we had to be careful, for there were times when they would set up a command post close by and run military exercises in this area. At this point the one who had the electronic sniffer warned us that we were coming into the area where we could be located with the motion sensing tracker so we stopped. There was an exact path that we had to follow to avoid detection and it was his job to get us past. So with patience we waited as he tested the air for any stray signals, and once satisfied signaled the "move out" and led us along a convoluted path until we were well inside. He then signaled that it was safe and we were past the border and now outside of the electronic tracking signals. Of course we were the enemy so we couldn't relax that much, still having to be on the alert for the random patrols, and stray dog teams that were sent out periodically. Luck was with us and because of the snowstorm raging most seemed to decide that it was better inside than out, and who could truly blame them?

Eventually we arrived at our destination, searched the surrounding area, and then with care entered into the home by the normal means of knocking on the door and being invited inside. With our arrival the storm had eased somewhat. With our search outside it was obvious as to why some official would covet this property. It was somewhat remote, the home, while old, was well built with plenty of room. A covered walkway and bridge that ran over a frozen creek that led one to a combination garage, workshop, and apartment that was built over the garage completed the layout. The views, even though with the weather we were facing made it impossible to see, were fabulous. I have to admit personally that it was very nice to get inside and out of that storm. Our team consisted of only three, both to remain hidden, and secondly not raise suspicions because of the number of people that arrived at this home. We appeared to be no more than relatives or friends visiting because of the holiday season.

Of course we placed our own devices before approaching the home to be sure that we had the area monitored. There was no way that we wanted to be approached without knowing. After all, all of us were quite aware of what would happen if we were caught. If we were lucky it would be a kangaroo court followed by prison, if not, torture and death. Of course none of this was known publicly since such would be protested throughout the world. So when one entered here one had better use every device, and every bit of training that was available to help guarantee success. So after the devices had been placed we headed away from the home and then approached it openly down their road on foot talking about the holiday and our anticipation of meeting our old friends. This, of course, to throw off any who might be observing the home, and we were sure that even with this nasty weather, someone would be.

So once inside the two members of my team took up their positions, one to watch through the windows, and the second to monitor our own hidden devices. I could see the nervousness on the faces of the family members, all four of them. The father took a deep breath and waited for me to speak. "Is all ready?" I asked.

"Yes, we have our packs together," was all he said.

I knew that he was waiting for the phrase that would confirm that we were the ones. After all there was a great possibility that we were the Secret Police trying to entrap them. And what better way than to get them to admit what was planned? I smiled and said, "Oh if it were summer, we'd be seeing and smelling those lovely roses. I know that your wife is famous for her roses," which, of course, she wasn't. In fact she had no talent for growing things at all. Her house plants very rarely survived and where they were located was called death row, since she killed them more often than keeping them healthy and alive. I heard the sigh of relief when they received the phrase. "Okay then, we need to move, and do it now." About the time I got those words out I heard the one who was monitoring our devices say, "Here they come. It looks like you were correct. From our devices I'm seeing at least three vehicles, and one helicopter."

I smiled as the ones approaching would be in for a surprise. Instead of coming in and taking a family who had no way to defend themselves, and with the weather so bad, which made me feel sorry for that pilot, they were going to run into a trap themselves. We'd leave our own mark on them before we left. Turning back to the family which consisted of the parents and two children, the oldest being a boy of about thirteen, I said, "Let's move. No more time to enjoy the season. It's now or never." They took a quick last look around, and I'll give them credit, they didn't hesitate at all but headed for the pathway that would lead across to the garage where we would then head into the forest and disappear. We originally hoped that we could do this without this government being the wiser, but we had dealt with Murphy too many times to expect it to go smoothly, and once again good old Murphy was here.

I had the one who had been watching out the windows to go with the family to the garage where we would all meet up. It was time to have some fun, so to speak. Although shooting at each other really isn't fun, but to give these some of their own we thought it was only right. So when we were sure that the family and our man was out of the house and on their way we waited until we saw, through the lightly blowing snow, the vehicles pull up and stop. We now could hear, above the blowing winds, the helicopter approaching. Giving it a few more minutes and time for the ones to exit their vehicles I opened the door and tossed a flash-bang their way just to let them know that things would not be going as they had planned. I almost laughed since they didn't know what was going on and when the flash-bang exploded it was like watching a stirred up ant nest with the Secret Police running in all directions trying to avoid whatever this explosion was.

You could hear the sharp rev of the engines and the change of pitch on the blades of the chopper as the pilot pulled up and changed his direction. But unknown to them or the pilot we had planned for this possibility and that chopper would not survive to return back to wherever it had originated from. I did not necessarily like to kill, but felt no qualms about these who had killed too many of the innocent. So I felt it only right that they got a little of what they dished out. The electronics expert looked and me and smiled. We both knew what was to follow, and the ones out there didn't have a clue. The flash-bang let the third member know that it would be time to get the next part moving, and once he heard us firing he would do his part.

Looking over at the one who had smiled I nodded and asked, "Are you ready?" Still with that wicked smile on his face he only nodded. "Okay, let off the clip and let's get out of here." We both did, but really it was only for show, something to slow the ones outside down. And to add to their problems we were jamming their communications so that they couldn't ask for reinforcements on what was to be a routine pickup. Now moving towards the exit we had about 15 seconds before the next phase began, and before we reached the door it began. These ones on the outside were in for a big surprise, yes another one. And it began with a series of explosions one shutting down the road into the property isolating them here until help could arrive, which would be long after we were gone.

We finally made the garage and the helicopter came sweeping in out of the snowstorm coming too close which triggered one of our automatic devices that sent a small missile, one that would normally do minor damage to a target because of its small size, but this time Murphy was on our side and it struck something vital that caused the chopper to ignite. We never knew what but suddenly the chopper was in flames and the surprised pilot had put the nose down in reaction, and this was followed by the chopper crashing into the house, leading to an explosion that knocked us over, collapsing the covered bridge and walkway between the now flaming ruins that had been the house and the garage where we were located. Throwing debris in every direction, and actually destroying the vehicles, since they were parked too close to that house. As to injuries or deaths to the ground forces, we had no idea and really didn't care.

All of us stood back up stunned for a moment, but only that. We quickly headed back into the wilderness and disappeared into that snowstorm, knowing that officially it would be reported that the family had perished in the explosion and fire. A few hours later we were back across the border and into our hidden vehicles heading back to our homes where we could celebrate Christmas with our families. Yes we had provided a wonderful gift for this family and while they were silent you could see that they were almost afraid to believe that they were safe.

The irony in all of this was that the nation that we had just snatched this family from, had, at one time, been a shining light for freedom. They had helped bring down governments less suppressive than the one that now ruled. But somewhere along the time line, the citizens got lazy, got complacent, and just let things go, and now they were paying a price for their indifference. This nation had become the new USSR, and had become as closed as that fallen nation ever had been. This used to be the United States of America, but its name might as well be written this way – "United States of Amerika", since it more reflected its nature now. And we were their neighbor to the North – Canada, at one time working together as friends, but now enemies.

The All Powerful

Author's Notes

I've had the opportunity, if one wants to call it that, to have lived through interesting times. I was in high school when President Kennedy was assassinated. Watched as a president and vice president resigned, and we had the first president that wasn't elected to office. Lived through the attempt to impeach a president, see another shot in an assassination attempt, and see the two towers collapse after a successful terrorist attack. And this is just the high, or low if you prefer, lights.

Yet through most of this we, this nation, remained who we were. Unfortunately, in the background there were many changes taking place that would change the leadership of this nation and move it closer to what Europe's preferred government is. They have been attempting to do this for as long as this nation has existed, and finally succeeded in taking over one of the major parties and getting their chosen person into the White House.

And with the press imitating Pravda we suffered through eight years of lawlessness, and corruption on an unbelievable scale that went all the way to the highest office. Fixed elections, and the disappearance of important members of the government, with one failure after another from our leadership, it appeared that we were about to disappear from the world stage as we moved closer into the direction and the ways of the old USSR. (Welcome to Amerika!)

Of course this is my opinion, and others have theirs. Still it was with these thoughts and what I was witnessing that led to this short story. And by stating what I have here then this story will probably make much more sense.

The All Powerful

It was quiet in his office as he sat behind the huge desk. The only item sitting on the desk was a pen set from a friend, well this person had been a friend, but no longer associated with him – especially since he had taken office through rigged elections in the past. Yet, this past term had been a wonderful time, as he and his cronies, with the press's support of course, twisted the laws of this country to fit their own ideas of how it should be. In many ways, he was close to the most powerful leader in the whole world and he enjoyed this position tremendously. After all, who could challenge him? As he glanced past the pen set, there was the standard desk calendar, and a pad to make writing easier, and the clean empty desk, he knew that as well as it had gone he hadn't been sworn in for that second term, yet.

The sunlight was streaming through the windows that were directly behind him, but if someone wanted to remove him, he would be safe here, since the glass was more than bullet proof. So it was easy to swivel his chair around and look out on a pastoral scene which reflected the false peace that the manicured lawns, flower beds, and trees reflected. After all, another election had come and gone, and he was still in power, still free to do as he pleased, free to make his will the law of the land. Not some old musty document that didn't apply to this world, his world. Of course he had won again by fraud. But there would be none to challenge him. After all he controlled not only the press, but all law enforcement and the military. The highest courts were his to command, and the underhouses, these elected officials were ineffective and couldn't see their way out of a brown paper sack, let alone challenge his abuses. He laughed quietly.

It had worked perfectly. And the field tests were out in the open for all to see, and so easily explained away. It had been in the past that the weak points in these elections were pointed out to him. And at that point he put the best minds to work, the programmers that were of like mind, and they worked and tested. Then when it came time for this new election, they put the software into the electoral system, and specifically where it would be to his advantage, and ran those field tests – all successful. It was easy to explain away why votes were going to him, no matter how someone voted. "Oh the machines just need some calibration that's all." And it was believed. Then the front end was put into place giving the illusion that the votes were going to the ones the citizens had chosen to vote for. But in the background with the algorithm in place, behind the scenes actually changing the votes to him, it became fun to watch.

He played at campaigning, and even though he had that one slip with that damn open mic before the campaigning, before the elections, the statement of "when" instead of "if" I win the election had been heard by all, but the press said nothing, did nothing, or just ignored his statement. He had told that leader that once he was re-elected, and that was all but guaranteed, that the gloves would come off and he could do as he pleased. He knew that if anybody had chased down that slip they may have been able to stop his plans, to discover the fraud, at that point. So easy, to exploit that weak spot in the system, a system that really had many. He had watched, in the past, as a particular region had done their voting, but the race was close, and the challenger won. When a recount was demanded and given, when the chosen candidate hadn't won a second term, all of a sudden votes were coming out of the woodwork, from hidden places, votes that supposedly were not counted, and funny thing, all these votes were for the losing candidate until there was enough for her to win back her position. And not one question from the "sheeple", not one. It made it obvious that such could be done on a national scale and with his control of every aspect of not only the election and press, but the government no one would question the outcome.

But he had to admit that he had a rather large ego, and so he wanted this challenger to feel like he would win, only to be crushed in the end. *But I had to be careful then, since the winning margin couldn't be too great.* Then and only then would he tally full satisfaction from the many demeaning, well demeaning in his mind, facts that this one had brought into the open. And as the polls closed across this large country, one by one, the challenger appeared to be winning, building his confidence that all that money, all that hard work, all that campaigning was paying dividends, only to be crushed at the end when it all swung to him, the incumbent, the present leader. And it was with much satisfaction and a salve to his ego when he saw his challenger realize that he had failed. *Yes, so satisfying.* Still there was much to do, so very much to do to change this country, to make himself the permanent leader, and with so many years ahead of him, in his mind, he once again laughed – for who could stop him?

Oh yes it had been a great time to watch this unfold, and in private, he rewarded those like-minded programmers that made this happen, and made it happen just as he had envisioned. The software did its work and then removed itself leaving no trace behind. Those camps were built, the brown-shirts were being trained, soon, yes very soon the reality of his grand plan would be known to all, and especially any who had challenged him, any who were against him. After all, like the Romans of the past, he would become the permanent leader, the emperor, and make the government god that the "sheeple" would be required to worship, or pay a hard price. Yes it was all coming together, and there were none, absolutely none who could challenge him. And it really was too bad about those programmers, after all who could have foreseen that accident. And with that thought, he quietly laughed once again.

The Move

Author's Notes

This one, like, "The Great Break", was written for a writing contest. In this case I did submit it. The word count limitation on this one was one thousand five hundred words. To me that's not much to work with. Of course back in elementary school this would be something to sweat over as it would be much too long. After coming back to it much later and rereading it I know there was no way for it to go anywhere. Of course I've reworked it since otherwise it wouldn't be here.

Here we follow a young couple through the eyes of the wife, and the next door neighbors. In this limited scope we learn a bit of her history, and the fact that she's recently with child. And this weighs on her mind as well has her relationship with her man. And also she's trying to make a good impression on her neighbors.

We must remember that everything that happens to us must be interpreted by us. So whatever we see, feel, hear, etcetera, is influenced by who we are, our history, what we are doing at that very moment, and our very heredity. What this means is the fact that whatever the event it will always be slightly different for everybody.

In Police Science they use the example of a park scene where you have a number of people enjoying their time there. A purse is snatched, and there are plenty of witnesses. Yet the statements from those witnesses are different, and many times conflict and contradict each other.

It was with these thoughts that this story came about. Many times what we believe to be real turns out to be our imagination in the end. You know, "Things that go bump in the night".

The Move

It felt great to have made the move out of that small dingy apartment into this more spacious one. Well, at least it felt that way if it truly wasn't. The place appeared to be brighter, cleaner, and definitely newer than the place that they had left. Smiling happily as she looked down at her growing abdomen, she could just see the changing shape as the baby grew inside of her. Looking up at her husband she teasingly said. "Look what you've done to me. Now I'll never have that sexy figure that attracted you to me in the first place."

Laughing, he playfully swatted her behind and said. "Now, that's just not true. I love all of you, and that includes what you are adding to this family. And your changing shape just makes me love you more, and I really couldn't be happier." He frowned, "I just wish that I didn't have to be away so much. I mean with so little time together I am surprised that you're pregnant. And I have yet to meet any of our neighbors." He paused briefly and with a smile he continued, "Yeah I know, I'm usually away when they are here, and it's quite the opposite when I'm home." Shrugging, he said, "Oh well, such is the life of the working class hero." He bent over and kissed her heartily, and somewhat lustfully, sighed and said, "I do have to leave, even though I want to stay and enjoy all of you."

Laughing she replied, "I know, I know, but I haven't been able to find a job yet, and even though my pregnancy isn't that far along, few want to hire someone that will be leaving for a baby sometime in the near future. So I guess we really don't have a choice on this. But . . ." She said as she hugged him hard, "I really, really do miss you when you are gone. Now get out of here before I beg you to stay." She saw him to the door and then as he left, slowly closed it, sighed, and thought, *I miss him already, and now I won't see him for a few weeks. I guess I knew what I was getting into when he asked me to marry him. Heck, we had been dating for over a year, and I knew exactly how it was going to be.* This didn't make it any easier when he had to go. And it just seemed like it took too many days, hours and minutes until he was back in her arms. *Oh well, in a few hours that nice next door neighbor Mr. Samuels, and his wife, oh what's her name? Oh that's right, Kellie . . . anyway they will be coming over to visit – to help welcome us to the new neighborhood. Well then, I better make sure this place is presentable.*

Ceri quickly cleaned the small apartment so that it would be presentable for company, and finished dressing. The couple had promised that they would give her a tour of the gardens that were close by. And they had said that the sight was well worth the time. Besides, one got to exercise, even if it was just walking. And while this would be her first child, she knew that exercise was important. She also knew, from observation, as she entered her third trimester, that exercise would be the last thing on her mind. Just as she finished everything there came a knock on the door. Taking a deep breath, because she really didn't know them yet, and at the same time wanting to make a good impression, she got herself in order, opened the door, and with enthusiasm and a big smile said. "Hi! I'm ready, if you are."

The two standing at the door looked at each other and then at her with Kellie saying, "Great! We've been looking forward to this. And it's a sunny warm day out there. So, I'm sure that the birds will be singing and we will have a wonderful time."

Looking again at both of them once again trying to hide her nervousness, she said, "Okay! Then let's go."

Over an hour later she was back full of smiles. They had been right, the gardens were beautiful, and seemed to just go on forever. The day was bright, sunny, with a soft cool breeze and the birds were singing up a storm. It seemed so peaceful and invigorating all at the same time. She was only sorry that Jesse, yes that was Mr. Samuels' first name, had to leave. Still Kellie was great at pointing out everything that was there to see. Well, it was time to relax a little then finish the unpacking, followed by a lonely lunch, but maybe as she got to know the couple it would not be so.

* * *

"So what do you think?" Jesse asked. "That's if you have the time right now."

"About what? The day? The gardens?" Then Kellie paused smiling, as she leaned on the desk in front of her, "or everything in general?"

He laughed, "Now that's one of the many reasons I married you – your sense of humor." He leaned back placing his hands behind his head, "So sorry that I had to leave today. I so wanted to go through the gardens with the two of you." He leaned forward asking, "Did it go well?"

* * *

Even though she was early in her pregnancy she felt a little tired and decided that after lunch she would take a nap. She laughed at this since as a kid she always fought her parents over doing this. *At least this apartment is starting to shape up*, she thought. But she had to admit that the bed was looking awfully good.

* * *

"Oh I have a few seconds before I have things I must do, so I guess the answer is yes."

"So what's your impression of our new neighbor?" Jesse asked.

Kellie, looking down at her watch realized that she needed to leave and interrupted saying, "We'll have to continue later, not enough time to go into that now. A statement on something light and simple yes, but on this subject no. I've really got to go. See you tonight?"

Smiling Jesse said, as he looked down at his overloaded desk, "I can hardly wait, but I have too much paperwork that needs to be brought up to date and it will keep me here and probably late. So reality pushes in once again, but sometime tonight, it's a date for sure."

* * *

For the next couple of weeks she went on daily walks with the couple next door and found that she was looking forward to both the walks and the company. It was nice to get out of that apartment and have someone to talk to. With her husband on that run she would have been alone, and she really hated it. So these times out in the bright warm sunshine, listening to the birds, the small talk between Kellie and Jesse, which reminded her of similar conversations between she and her man – idyllic days for sure, which helped fill those lonely days, leaving her happy, if not missing her man even more, helped. It was still at least two weeks before he returned and with those walks she was slowly learning the area. She had so much to tell him when he got back, saying so to her neighbors. The two looked a bit puzzled but accepted what she said.

* * *

Later that same day, as Kellie and Jesse met in the office, discussing work, he said, "That young woman, who is in the apartment next to us, seems so normal, leaving one to wonder why she's here."

"Ceri?" She asked.

"Yes. Anyway, who'd have guessed that everything she is seeing is an illusion – a fantasy. When her husband died in that traffic accident, which she witnessed, it almost destroyed her. We were told that she isn't a strong person. And that pregnancy of hers is from artificial insemination, since he died before she became pregnant. After his death she just went off the deep end into this fantasy world she's created – separating herself from her friends and family – leading to her being placed here. In fact it was her friends that alerted us to what was happening with her. They said she'd been lingering, after work, around that fertility clinic. And then when she had announced her pregnancy to her friends and she and her husband were so looking forward to the time when the child was born they felt things had gone too far. I know that she believes that we are her next door neighbors, and that her husband is alive, and the child she's carrying is theirs, but, in truth, this is a mental facility and even though she doesn't understand or realize it, we are her caretakers."

The Great Break

Author's Notes

There are writing contests everywhere. And, of course, to enter one must stay the course and keep the word count down. I guess I can say when I began this journey keeping the word count down wasn't so difficult. In fact my first Christmas short story was less than a thousand words. I have to admit that that was just about the last time. Part of what these contests are for is the revenue that it generates which helps the company to stay afloat. It also forces writers to really work hard on their particular manuscript to keep it within the rules.

In this case the maximum words allowed were two thousand, and here you were given a word which you had to use as the key to your submission. And that word was "break". (Let me say that my intention was to submit this short story to the contest, but in the end I didn't have the funds to be able to do so.) So I thought about this word for a while and as I like to do I approached it from a different direction.

We hear it all the time, "Time waits for no one." And honestly it's true. It's our perception that determines whether it flies or goes slow. Of course, if we were able to travel the speeds that are taken for granted in the Science Fiction novels then time would slow and we would live longer. If we think about the many civilizations that have risen and fallen over time, there is no guarantee that ours will survive. And when civilization collapses there are always periods of chaos and anarchy before reason and stability returns leaving the past many times completely unknown to the ones living in their present.

It was with these thoughts, and of course, that imagery that this story came to me – and if just flowed. As expected, like all manuscripts, it required editing. And the neat thing for me is the fact it was under that word count limit at the time of writing – rare I have to admit.

The Great Break

We only knew it by the slang, "the breaks". And when one took the time to go out and locate it, where the "great" came from nobody knew. In the area the lands were more or less wilderness and somewhat flat until you reached a dip or drop of the land, which wasn't really wide, but it was the only change. Once one crossed then it rose up once again and you were back to those flat lands. Yeah, the area was covered in trees, and all sorts of wild shrubs except the great break. Nothing grew there, and if one thought it might have been a channel for water, well there was no sign water had ever ran there. So the title for this small depression became more of a joke.

We are a people who use iron tools, and are farmers and such and none of us could even remember when the great break hadn't existed. Like the great forests that were beyond our realm it had always been in our lore, in our memory. My friend Jon who loved to explore – when we could get away from the work that we always faced – treated the breaks as a minor annoyance and dismissed it as unimportant. Still, if one wanted to have food over the winters then work we must, and no one wanted to see their women and children hungry. If he was asked about what he thought, he'd simply shake his head. "Nothing important there. I will never understand why this little line in the ground is so important."

Of course none of us had explored it too far in either direction as it paralleled our lands. And the few times we had been beyond and had gone deep into that wilderness we found nothing other than much the same. Yeah we were isolated, which allowed us some protection. We had traveling merchants that brought what we couldn't make ourselves, and buy our surpluses. I remember Jon saying to me, "Tim, without these traveling merchants we'd probably have to abandon our farms. While we can do for ourselves there will always be things we must have and if we do not then as the equipment wears out we will find our work more difficult until it reaches a point where we can no longer function. And when that happens then our land will return to the forest and there will be nothing here to even mark our passing."

I thought to disagree but hesitated for a moment and realized what he said had a ring of truth, so I said, "Jon, you're probably right." Still in my mind I would always go back to the mystery surrounding *the great break*. I knew the risk we took with the traveling merchants, not that they didn't take risks themselves. There were always raiders, highwaymen, thieves and murderers who wanted what they had as well as anything we had. So trust was a fleeting thing, and the dangers were always high. If one of the known traveling merchants didn't show when they were scheduled then we would suspect they had met with foul play, which would increase the tension and our fear. After all information can always be extracted leading the bad to us.

In a sense it was such a situation that led to the discovery of why *the great break* was named as such. Fortunately, for us, the incident turned out to be a false alarm, and in the end all was okay . . . But at the time . . .

"Where is he, and his guards?" Jon asked. "He's a moon cycle late and he's never been this late. I really need, or I should say we need what he's bringing and this delay is costing us."

Our local metal worker agreed. "Yes, without the pieces he's bringing I can't complete the repairs and without those repairs we will fall further behind on our preparations – not good, not good at all."

What could I say when they'd summed it up so well. Turning to Jon I said, "Why don't you and I head out and down the trail a bit, head up to the ridgetop and see if we can catch any distant smokes or maybe catch a glimpse of their approach."

I could tell he was about to say something that would be against my suggestion, but he hesitated and after a moment spoke. "You know, that's probably not a bad idea. There's still plenty of daylight and we should be able to make the trek there, take time to search the area, and then return before dusk. Or at least not long after." He thought for a moment, "Okay, let's you and I do this Tim. Go get your bow and long knife, put together a little something and I'll go do the same. We'll meet back here in no more than a notch on the dial."

I nodded in agreement and went immediately to my home and with the help of my wife gathered what was necessary and immediately returned. Jon was waiting. "That was fast".

"Well, you know I like, when I have the time," Jon replied, "to explore. It's so we have places to go if we need to run and hide, or maybe on one of my searches I can find a source so we don't have to barter for it.

Because of this I always have a pack ready, as well as my weapons."

Inwardly I laughed as I always teased him that the reason he was always out and about lay in the fact that his children were a loud noisy lot and he always preferred the quiet. While he would always deny such an accusation he would admit to me privately that the silence of the forest did have a draw. It wasn't that his children were unruly. In fact they were well disciplined and put in an honest day's work. It was the fact they would be boisterous when they did anything, and everyone in the village knew where they were at any given moment.

As we left the village and headed down the hidden trail a sudden wind came up. And it was then things began to get strange. I don't know how to describe it, only it didn't feel right. I've had time to think about it, but even now I have no way to describe the feelings or the sense of the moment. This was followed by a mist that blotted out everything. Then the skies darkened and the air felt electric as if a storm of some magnitude was descending upon us. The winds increased and the sound of these winds through the trees were deafening. So much so we had to yell to be heard. "Where'd this come from?" I yelled. I noticed that it was becoming harder to see as if night was descending upon us. I saw Jon shrug. We both turned to head back since we really weren't that far from the village. But there was no trail, nothing was recognizable.

Jon looked around and had a look of consternation on his face. I'm sure mine wasn't much different. He came over to me with his hands on his hips. "Okay . . . I don't know what's going on, or where we are. We should only be a couple of marks on the sundial out of the village, yet this area is completely unfamiliar."

When he stated that it made me worry even more. He is the explorer for our village and knows the area for at least a day's travel all around our village. We weren't that far out – we really couldn't be. It was at that moment, as the skies lightened and it became quiet, I looked and saw the great break. Only it was now different. Jon had his back to it and I grabbed him by his shoulders, turned him around and pointed. He just stared, for which I couldn't blame him as I was doing the same. Not only was it different but much of the forest was gone and in its stead there were now grasslands. I turned around in a full circle and as far as I could see it was the same. "Where'd the trees go?" I asked.

Once again he shrugged. I knew that he didn't have an answer but I couldn't help myself. Together we hiked over to what was now a wall made of some unfamiliar substance. We touched it and it felt rough and cool to the touch. It had a height that came to about mid-chest. We boosted ourselves to the top where the surface seemed flat and wide. Looking out in the distance beyond the wall there seemed to be something that had been described to us, but none of us had ever seen. And the sounds reaching our ears were even stranger. While it sat in the distance, this city filled the skyline, and ran in all directions as far as we could see. It left both of us silent and in awe.

Looking down the other side of this wall we saw someone standing at the bottom. For this side the drop down was much greater. In fact had we continued and had simply jumped over the wall we would have been injured, if not killed. Whoever this was, watched us. We crouched down curious as to what this individual wanted. He seemed to be dressed most strangely and had the look of someone important. When he spoke his accent was strange, but because of the distance we couldn't understand him. So we yelled down to him to please repeat what he said. Unfortunately it was obvious he couldn't make out what we were saying either. Looking in both directions we could find no way down so in the end we couldn't talk. Eventually this stranger backed up when he realized we would be unable to talk, headed towards a really strange – well I don't know how describe it, and neither did Jon. Anyway whatever it was, once he was inside, it moved and we watched in awe as it disappeared.

Standing back up and looking at each other to be sure we weren't dreaming we both decided to walk this flat surface for a little distance. It was then we found writings on top of the wall. It simply stated: THE GREAT BREAK. THE CITY CAN GO NO FURTHER THAN THIS WALL. WHAT IS ON THE OTHER SIDE SHALL REMAIN AS IT HAS ALWAYS BEEN. We looked at each other, and then back at the city, followed by looking at the great grasslands that now were on our right. We climbed down off that wall and began to retreat back in the direction we had come when there was a great shaking knocking us off our feet. The winds began howling again and darkness fell – not the darkness of night, but the darkness of a cavern – and we then were hit by heavy rains. Climbing to our feet we began to run, but stopped realizing it had been fear driving us.

We remained where we were and waited. There wasn't anything else we could do. Then suddenly it was gone. We found ourselves on the hidden trail with *the great break* off to our right, that small depression we had always known. Looking up through the trees we could see that little to no time had passed, and we were dry. We now knew the truth of *the great break*, but did we dare tell others? Would they even believe us? Probably not. So we decided to never reveal what we were shown. And it is here in this journal I write these words, only to be read after my death. And for you who read the words herein I leave it to you to decide – Tim.

Holiday Short Stories

This is part two of this book of short stories. One of the reasons for doing this simply was because the mood and direction of these stories are different and are tied directly to specific holidays. Whereas the previous six are simply short stories, and exist to tell a story.

The holidays used in this section are from the USA. One of the personal lessons I learned a long time ago is that each country, each culture have their own important holidays or celebrations that are unique to them. And while the three holidays are celebrated in the western hemisphere, even here they can vary by culture and country.

They are; Halloween, which is celebrated on the last day of October, Thanksgiving, which is celebrated on the third Thursday of November, and Christmas, which is celebrated on December twenty-fifth. Each can be tied to traditions that are deep from the past, and have changed as cultures change over time.

Understand that other than the Halloween short stories presented here, the ones for the other two holidays are Christian based, and as such will reflect that religion. Oh and as a warning, as you read these stories dealing with Thanksgiving and Christmas, have some tissues handy. They will bring a tear of two your way. It's not that they are negative, yet they do approach this time of year from a different direction. These short stories will be presented in the order of the holidays, from Halloween to Christmas Enjoy – F. D. Brant

One Night Going Home

Author's Notes

In my seasonal stories I like to write the stories from a different direction or perspective. What I mean, since this one was written for Halloween, is to write something that will possibly send chills down your spine, but not be scary. Or, as in my Christmas stories, to deal with other realities people face. Or, as in Thanksgiving, present an unexpected direction and conclusion to the story.

In this story the road that the protagonist travels exists. And at times the fog can be so thick that you cannot see beyond the hood of your car. It can make what should be a simple drive into a nightmare as you strain to catch those broken white lines that mean you're still on the road. And this road goes deep into the backcountry with very few homes, and long lonely stretches of nothing but road, brush, and the wild animals that inhabit the wilderness, before entering a small rural town or two.

And yes, I did have imagery for this story before I wrote it. Yet, because I knew that I wanted to write this for Halloween, the story needed to lean in that direction. If one thinks about it, just because one has the pictures in their mind, at that point the story is wide open as to mood and direction. It is here where one's conscious mind takes over and moves the story in the direction the author desires.

One Night Going Home

It had been a tough day at work – one of those days where anything that could go wrong did. So when he finally got into his car and drove out of the parking lot, heading in the direction of home, he was quite glad that it was over. He only hoped that the rest of the week would be better – after all it could hardly miss. While traffic was always heavy, he was hoping for an uneventful commute. It was a crisp fall day with a heavy overcast that was barely above the ground. Everything was cold, damp, and with the grayness it would have been easy to feel down. But the workday was over and home was only a commute away, so how could he feel down? Then, as he had barely headed out of the parking lot, an alert came over the radio broadcasting a major incident. But, in truth, he hadn't been paying attention, so he missed the location. Taking a deep breath he hoped that it wasn't in his direction. It had been frustrating enough as it was, and he didn't need an accident added to it.

Of course, he thought, *it's Halloween. No wonder this has been such a weird and crazy day.* As he got an update on that major incident he realized that indeed it was on his route home – he'd need to find an alternate way if he wanted to get home at all. The radio had already reported that the traffic was backed up for miles, and while a detour had been set up, it was only a 2-lane blacktop road, not designed for this amount of traffic. It was then that he made his decision, not realizing that sometimes such simple choices can change one forever. There was a back way home but it would add at least an hour to his commute. Still, from the sounds of it, this would take less time than trying to work through that mess. So he dropped off the freeway well before the backup using the surface streets to work his way towards the road he knew would take him around the incident. Fortunately he was familiar with these city streets and by remaining on the less traveled ones he finally reached the one that he wanted. Within five miles he would be turning off onto that backcountry road that initially had a lot of traffic because of a small community that existed just outside of this city. Once past that point the traffic would magically vanish and from there he would probably be alone, with only an occasional car passing him in the opposite direction.

* * *

Fortunately, for him, it had gone well, and now, well past that small community, he could relax. He had to shut off the radio since reception was poor in this area – the surrounding hills blocked the signals. With darkness falling, after all it was fall and the days short, his luck ran out. A heavy fog drifted in obscuring everything. He should have realized that this would happen since there had been a low heavy gray overcast. It wasn't like this was the first time that he had ever driven in the fog, but for whatever the reason, this fog bank was especially heavy. He had to slow down to first gear, and even then he was coming close to stalling the motor – he probably could walk faster. He could barely see beyond the hood of his car and the white lines on the road were difficult to see. When one would disappear he had to strain to see the next one. With the surface of the road dark gray to black with no solid lines on the side of the road to assist him he had to be alert. It would be too easy, in this stuff, to drive off the road and not realize it until it was too late. Not good since many of the areas where this road headed were ravines and deep canyons.

He cursed these conditions under his breath because it would probably take him most of the night just to work through the fog and mist, heck he still had another day in this week to work. All he saw was the shifting grayness that his headlights refused to penetrate and hear the sounds of his idling motor with the slap of his wipers as they kept the windshield clear. As he concentrated hard on staying on the road his subconscious mind picked up, in the distance, an orange flickering glow that colored the fog. Eventually this penetrated his conscious mind since he was driving towards it. *Now what?* It almost looked like the type of color that a construction vehicle warning lights would use – different from an emergency vehicle. *Why would something like that be out here tonight?* Then he remembered that many times roads were repaired at night because of the light-to-no-traffic situation. But he hadn't heard of any such thing happening on this one, but had to admit that he really hadn't paid attention since he rarely traveled it. At least if there was roadwork he should have no problem getting by. At that moment he realized that he had yet to see any lights approaching him from the opposite direction. He was completely alone, just he, the road, and maybe a construction crew.

He suddenly realized that the flicker he was seeing wasn't steady. It had to be something else, but what? He continued to slowly work his way down the road and the orange flickering glow continued to get stronger. It suddenly struck him that this might be a fire. *Why would something like this be out here, especially in weather like this?* It was too damp to be a wild fire. *Has someone besides me taken this route and then crashed and having their car catch fire?* It surely was a possibility with this weather. So splitting his attention between staying on the road and attempting to locate the source of that glow he continued on. Eventually he pulled even with the glow and found that it was off to the right and down over the embankment. This reinforced his thoughts that he had earlier that someone may have crashed. He pulled over carefully, not wanting to drive off the shoulder of the road, or leave his vehicle partially on the road itself for someone else to hit. Once safely parked, he started his emergency flashers – *one can't be too careful.*

When he got out of his car he shivered. The air was chilled, damp, and it had been warm and comfortable in his car. He quickly went to his trunk and grabbed a heavier coat that he always kept there and shrugged into it. As expected, it felt cold and sent chills through his body. Quickly he got back into the car and let the heater warm him and the jacket, which only took a moment or two. Once back out he walked to the edge of the shoulder looking down towards that glow, but with the thickness of the fog it was still diffused and nothing definite could be seen. The air was completely still and the only movement he could see was the fog and mist as it drifted through the lights from the car. This movement gave an unreal, insubstantial feel, making it seem that he was on an island and nothing else existed but him and this fog. He took out his small flashlight looking at the road's edge trying to see if he could see where this car may have gone off the road – at least this was his conclusion at the moment. Yet in the areas he searched there was nothing to indicate that anything had left the roadway. *At least that orange flickering glow isn't growing. Is that a good sign or bad?*

With a loss of ideas he decided that he had to find a way down to where this flickering glow was and began to look for a way down. Some distance ahead of where he parked there appeared to be a way down. When looking back he could barely see his headlights, as the fog had dimmed them to the point that one could tell that there were 2 lights but that was just about all. Here he carefully half slid, half hiked down the steep embankment slightly skinning his hands on the loose soils, which left them with a burning sensation. He dropped down what seemed to be a great distance and eventually reached what appeared to be a somewhat flat area. What's this, he thought, as he shined the light from the flashlight on the surface where he was presently standing. *This appears to be a trail or something. As far as I know there's nothing like this anywhere around here.* When he was younger he used to hike these hills and it was one of the reasons he was familiar with this road. In all that time, if he had his location correct, and he was sure that he did, he had never seen or been on a trail like this. *What is going on?*

With this trail, which seemed wider than he expected, it was easier to walk. Puzzled he asked, "How'd I ever miss this?" Shrugging, he had no answer. He began to trace his way back towards that orange flickering glow, and as he approached the area the fog lifted just enough to reveal a campfire. This was strange, why would there be such a thing here, it made no sense. Then glancing around where the light from the fire was touching he stopped in his tracks. He had to be dreaming. The last time he had seen anything even close to this had been the "Hitch" that had traveled across country like they used to do, but this was one of those old Conestoga wagons that one always sew in those old westerns. It showed much usage. The "Hitch" had been a promotion by a magazine as they traveled from the east coast to the west coast using just an ordinary wagon and horses. Of course they had a great support staff, something that the ones from the past did not. *What is this one doing here?* Once the shock of this ended he realized that there were people standing around the fire dressed somewhat strangely. Then he smiled remembering it was Halloween and these people had to be dressed in costume.

With the light from the fire he shut off his small flashlight placing it back in his jacket pocket – *never know how long the batteries will last,* and announced that he was here and if they needed any help. He could see that they were a bit nervous and the one he took for the father was holding what appeared to be a repeating rifle like the ones he had seen in those same old westerns. In this case it appeared to be well worn, but at the same time well cared for. There was a woman and four children, with the children ranging in age of what he figured to be 4 to roughly 9 years of age. All their clothes looked to be homespun. He stood at the edge of the firelight waiting to be invited in. After all this was their fantasy so he didn't want to invade it unless invited.

The man, after looking him over carefully, had a puzzled look on his face, but remained silent for a moment or two longer. "Are you alone?" He asked.

His accent seemed strange – definitely not someone from these parts. "Yeah, I'm alone." Again this was becoming stranger as time seemed to stop. *Who are these people?*

Taking a deep breath the man said, "Yeah come on in. I'm Jake and this here's my wife Emma, and these are our children as if you hadn't figured that out. So what are you doing out here on a night like this and unarmed?"

Unarmed? What does he mean unarmed? And furthermore what's this question about being alone? He found that the longer he remained here with them the more questions he had. "Oh I guess this is a safe enough area."

"Maybe so, but are you on foot? If not, how'd you get here?"

"Oh I left my car up above and it won't take me long to get back to it." He looked around and realized that one of the wheels on the wagon was broken and it seemed that they were stranded. He asked, "Is this why you're here, this broken wheel?"

Jake shrugged before speaking. He looked back at that broken useless wheel saying, "Yeah. We have a spare to replace it but not the bodies to do it. Emma and I can use the lever to lift the wagon to get the wheel off the ground but the children aren't big enough to brace it. If this had happened before we left the train then it wouldn't have been an issue. 'Nough bodies to fix it then, but it had to wait until we were well separated to break. So now we're stuck. Are you willing to help us? We need to get to the coast where we will meet other members of the family. They've said that there's some great land that we can take next to theirs."

This is getting stranger by the moment. I wonder if they are just practicing and trying to stay in character, or, well, who knows? I surely don't. But they are stuck and if I can help, why not? "Yeah, I can help. What do you need me to do?" He could see the relief in the man's eyes.

"Actually your part is easy, more or less. Once Emma and I have the wagon levered up just brace it so that it will stay up. Then we, you and I, can get that broken one off and replace it."

"Okay, let's do it. I need to get home, and back to work tomorrow. So the sooner we can get this accomplished the quicker I can be on my way." With directions from Jake he assisted them and after a couple of hard hours, which he found himself sweating, they got the broken wheel off and the new one mounted. Breathing hard from the work he still smiled inwardly. He had never tackled anything like this and it felt good to have helped. Still it was getting really late and he needed to get home, and once there a quick shower. At least tomorrow would be Friday and even though he knew that he would be tired he could muddle through. He saw the gratitude in their eyes as he took his leave.

Jake asked if there was anything they could do for him, and he told them no. Jake then asked, "Can you at least tell us your name? I mean we gave you ours that way we know who to thank."

Smiling he said, "Just call me Bill, everybody else does."

At this point Jake came over grabbing his hand shaking it strongly. "Well, thank you Bill. Without your help I just don't know what we would have done. God Bless."

Embarrassed Bill smiled, "You are most welcome. But I do have to go. Good luck." He retraced his steps and was quickly out of the light from the small campfire. He reached back into his pocket taking out the small flashlight once again, realizing that he hadn't used it while they had been replacing that wheel. Turning he saw them watching him until the fog obscured them. He heard Jake say as they disappeared, "Strange, never saw anyone dressed like that, and to be unarmed, unexpected. I didn't know that people lived around here, and what was it he called his horse?" There was a brief silence and he heard Jake once more say, "Strange, really strange."

Bill thought the very same thing; it had been a very strange evening so far. Eventually he located the point where he had come down from the road, carefully worked his way back, then down the shoulder of the road to his still idling car. It was as he had left it. He looked over the side once again, but the glow from that fire had become invisible. It didn't matter, he still had miles to go, and the fog still seemed heavy. Sighing he climbed back in and continued his drive. Fortunately within a couple of miles the fog lifted, then disappeared, and he could see a beautiful full moon giving the surrounding country a ghostly quality that fit right into the night that it was – Halloween.

* * *

That weekend, curious, he went to a local historical library. He had related his story on Friday and everybody at work had racked it up to his imagination or an elaborate Halloween prank. Yet, the incident had stayed with him. So on Saturday he was now looking through old diaries from the late 1800's. From their dress and what little he knew of what he saw he figured that it had to have been from that time. In this section he eventually located a diary written by a woman who with her husband and four children had come into this region around 1886 to 1888. He learned that she and her husband Jake Sorenson had come into the area in the fall of that year, separating from the wagon train that they had been a part of, heading towards the coast where family had been waiting – only to have a wheel break when it fell into a hole. They had been there a couple of days trying to solve the problem that they had faced and it looked like they would have to abandon their wagon and proceed on foot. In fact that was what would have happened the next day. But that night a miracle happened.

He stopped at this point as chills ran up and down his spine, *No this cannot be right. It's just not possible, not at all.* Yet before him in her handwriting was the description of a stranger coming into their camp in a heavy fog at night who was alone, on foot, and dressed strangely. One who had been unarmed – unheard of at this time, and when leaving, disappearing into that same fog, who had said his name was Bill. He had assisted in the replacement of their broken wheel and was never seen again. It had allowed them to continue on and meet up with family.

He slowly placed it back on the shelves, and immediately drove back out on that road trying to locate the very spot where he had pulled off. After a few hours of searching he finally saw his tracks from two days before, here he stopped, and could actually see his shoe tracks still imprinted in the soils. It had been a wet fog so the ground had been also and when it had dried had set his tracks. He followed them to where he had left the roadway and looked over the side. He saw the marks he left as he had descended. Below all he could see was brush. There was no sign of that trail that he had hiked that Halloween night. No sign that there had ever been such a thing. He stood there staring. *Just what happened that night?* He felt that suddenly he was in one of those episodes of "Twilight Zone". He had no other explanation. If it hadn't been collaborated by that diary then he could have chalked it up as a dream, maybe a fantasy.

Again those chills ran up and down his spine. Somehow that fog had allowed a window into the past. With the need of that family being great, somehow the barriers had come down and he had helped them, but had he really? Had he traveled back in time to help a family in need? He knew that it was something for which he would never have an answer. Slowly he returned to his car, continuing to stop and look over the embankment looking for that trail and only seeing the brush, eventually giving up he drove back home. He had to admit that it was something that would be with him the rest of his life – something that defied explanation. Shaking his head, he thought, *Halloween, who'd have thought?*

Breakdown

Author's Notes

I grew up in the country. We had a two mile dirt road that led out to what we have always called, "the ranch". In the winter, many times, the road became impassable. We've buried more cars over the years than I can count – Which meant, at a later time, we would have to return with shovels and such, dig them out, get them unstuck, and hopefully be able to get them home.

It was a rough life, but honestly I wouldn't trade it for a life in the city, even though presently that's where I live. The one thing it taught you are self-sufficiency. Not that we particularly enjoyed being out in the cold and rain, being covered in mud as the wheels spun, throwing up great gobs of mud and water, spraying you as you pushed and rocked the car trying to get it to move.

At times, when we'd have to hike home, it would be a full moon night, with a heavy damp fog obscuring everything. With the moonlight filtering through, the fog continually thinning, thickening, and moving, with the constant drip of moisture off the brush, the world around one would become eerie and spooky. This would lead the imagination to create things moving in that fog.

With these experiences, over time, I began to develop a story that we used on Halloween. We'd create haunted walks on the property, and when we would bring the people in for the walk I'd tell a story or two to set the mood. And while this isn't quite the same story there are many elements within it that can be traced back to those beginnings.

Breakdown

It was one of those early fall evenings – cool, crisp, and a full moon making all the surrounding land appear magical. One could almost imagine a fairy tale scene as they headed home in their car. As they climbed the hills on the freeway they knew that soon home would be beckoning and after a tough work week they could finally relax.

Pulling off the freeway at the off ramp, the same that they had for the last ten years, all was familiar. Jessie commenting as he shook his head said, "Now this was a tough week, and I truly cannot wait until we get home. I have to admit I'm exhausted and am ready for some quiet time, how about you?"

Bill, his older brother, thought a minute before replying and thinking that it was not unusual for them to put in ten to fourteen hours a day just to keep the business going. Heck, even driving was almost enough to put him to sleep, and he was driving. "I have to agree with you there, Jessie. I'm beat, and in truth, I am looking forward to this weekend. You know we probably put in somewhere around eighty hours each this week."

Home, always such a wonderful word, was an isolated piece of property out in the middle of nowhere. It had been in the family for a couple of generations. Laughing as he thought about it Jessie could remember when one of his high school teachers had to bring him home. They always had problems, when growing up, with missing school because there were times that the dirt road they lived on became impassible. There was very few living like that so most of the time there was just disbelief. But that all changed when that teacher, who was a drama teacher, had to take him home. This teacher would then tell a tall tale about his trip out to their home – it went something like this:

"Well when I took this student home I really didn't think much about it – even when he stated that he lived pretty far out in the country. After all, we have a number of students who say the same thing. But to my surprise I was not prepared in any way for this trip. Let tell you, they are really isolated there.

"Now you drive on an isolated blacktop road as far as you can go. From there it changed to dirt . . . dirt – no problem, I thought. But eventually the road became so bad that I was barely creeping along, you could walk faster. Then I had to switch to a Jeep that was parked there for that purpose, followed by mules, as the road became so bad the jeep couldn't go any farther. Then even the mules couldn't go any further, leaving us on foot and using ropes to help us over the steep parts. Eventually I saw where this student lived. Isolated would be an understatement."

It was interesting that after the teacher had brought him home that one time that they never had problems again about missing school. And yes, while the story was a large exaggeration, which he was sure continued to grow with time, there still was some truth in there. Smiling to himself and shaking his head in the remembrance he knew that they were now approaching the beginning of that dirt road. Looking out to the west he saw that the fog was rolling in and probably before they got home it would be over them obscuring everything. This time of year it would be very wet, so he was thankful he was in a warm dry car.

Bill, relaxing a bit once they reached the road stated, "You notice, at least for me anyway, that once we hit this road that it seems that all the pressures of the city just seem to start vanishing and it's like a large weight is being lifted off. It happens every time, but at the same time until I get here I don't even realize that those pressures are there. For me it's the first sign that we are close to home. Only about four to five miles to go and it's over for a couple of days."

"Yeah, I have to agree as it seems things just roll off me when we hit this final stretch. Really never thought of it that way but you're right. Different subject, but how are you and your girlfriend doing? I know with the hours we put in its difficult to find time for us let alone girlfriends. I know with mine, this lifestyle you and I are presently living, frustrates her. She feels that I don't spend enough time with her." Shrugging he continued, "But what can I do? I mean right now while we are successful, and there's more work than the two of us can do. We just aren't quite in the place to be able to hire anyone else. Close, yes, but not quite yet."

"Yeah, know what you mean. I really never thought the business would take off like it did. And your assessment of our situation is quite correct. Even what you say about your girlfriend seems to apply to me also. Yeah, Leah is quite unhappy about it, but has to admit . . . what the heck was that?"

The car made a sudden lurch then a funny sound and then it was like the engine was not connected to anything. "Oh no!" Bill exclaimed, "I think we just dumped the transmission."

"You're kidding right? I mean the last thing I want

to do tonight is walk the last two miles home, especially now that that fog has reached us. Did you try any of the other gears?"

"Yeah, and even reverse, we have nothing." Then sighing he continued, " And of course here there is no signal for the cell phones, until we get home and even there the signal can be very iffy. Better get the flashlight out of the glove box, and we can look under the hood, but I don't think we can fix this one."

Jessie said, "Okay . . . ah here it is. Have you checked it lately?" Turning it on while looking into the lens he was momentarily blinded. Shaking his head he asked, "Now why do we do that? I mean why is it that when we want to check a flashlight we look into it like that?"

Laughing his brother replied, "You know I really don't know, but we all do it. Shall we see if there is anything we can do? I really do not want to stay here all night."

"Me either, and walking doesn't appeal to me either, but I think, as you said, there is no choice."

They got out and propped the hood open. Looking into the engine compartment they felt the heat coming off the motor. There was a smell of hot transmission fluid, and a little smoke from where it had hit the exhaust system. Shining the flashlight down Jessie saw what looked like a puddle developing under the car. "Hey Bill, look under the car where I have the light and see if you can see if what I am seeing is just a shadow or something from the car."

Bill then looked under the car where the light was hitting the ground and groaned, "It's transmission fluid alright – looks like we at least blew the seals. But I suspect from the sound that it was everything. That's going to cost us at least three grand to fix." He got up and came around to the front of the car and then said, "I guess that seals it, ha ha, play on words, so to speak. Might as well start walking, this car's going no further tonight."

Jessie, starting to pull his hand with the flashlight out from under the hood, close to the motor, touched something hot, jerked his hand in reaction, and in the process the flashlight left his hand and went flying, and hit a rock and then broke. "Great, now we have to depend on the moonlight. You don't have another one do you?"

Shaking his head no Bill said, "No such luck . . . I figured one would be enough. Well at least there's a full moon, and even with this fog we can see the road pretty clearly."

* * *

Once away from the car they found it deathly quiet. There was no breeze, just the drifting fog and the sound of moisture dripping off the surrounding brush. At times they could see a little distance ahead of themselves only in the next second to have the fog close in on them with gray wisps, creating shadows giving the appearance of something moving just out of sight, followed by the fog completely closing in allowing them to see nothing. The dirt road remained easy to follow, as it was a lighter strip to the eyes. "Did you hear that?" Jessie asked. Stopping, they both listened carefully, but other than the steady dripping moisture they heard nothing. Shaking his head Jessie said, "I swore I heard something going through the brush, but I guess it was my imagination."

"Maybe, but it still could have been a rabbit or even a bobcat. They all are out here and as you know night is their time."

"True, didn't think of that. Anyway let's get home; I'm quite ready to get out of this." Jessie shivered involuntarily, but didn't speak, signaling to continue.

Once again they started out and then both looked at each other as they heard something moving in the brush. Once again they stopped and it stopped. "I heard it this time also, Jessie. But why would it stop when we stop? Are we starting to let our imaginations run away here?"

"I don't know, but it sure can send shivers up your spine and make those short hairs stand up on the back of your neck that's for sure."

"Agreed, let's get home we aren't going to solve this here, and probably it's just some small animal anyway and the starting and stopping is just coincidence." Once again they continued their walk and as they did the sounds of movement in the brush reached their ears. After a number of pauses and starts with the sounds in the brush starting and stopping with them they knew it was something more . . . but what? So far there had been no hostile move just the unnerving mimicking of their movement. Again no breeze, just silence in this eerie world with the moonlit fog continually shifting, adding illusions of ghosts, the sounds of the constant dripping, and the movement of something in the brush, all keeping them company and on edge.

They picked up their pace and as they did so did the unknown watcher in the brush. But at no time did the sound approach any closer, or retreat. It became a constant companion making the brothers on edge and extremely nervous. Eventually as they climbed the last hill they saw the gate that led into the property and was thankful, as they knew that within five minutes they would be in the yard and their dogs would be barking out friendly greetings. Then the tension they were feeling would be evaporating, and probably in the morning they both would laugh about what was transpiring tonight. Yet even as they passed through the gate knowing that there was fencing out from the gate in both directions the sounds in the brush continued to follow. How was it possible? They figured that if whatever it was to continue to follow that here it would have to enter the road to go around the fence and maybe they would have a chance to spy what this creature was that was following them . . . it didn't. Somehow it went over the fencing and continued to follow and remained their companion all the way down the hill and into their yard. Instead of the friendly greeting that they had expected from their dogs, they could hear them whimpering, and when they saw them the two dogs had their tails between their legs showing fear.

This heightened the threat. This was the last thing that they had expected. They decided to head inside the house and get that shotgun just in case whatever had been following them was hostile. As they entered the house they tried the light switch but the power was dead. "What the heck?" Bill asked.

Jessie looked at him questionably, "No lights?"

Shaking his head Bill said, "No power, I guess, time

to light the kerosene lantern." He walked slowly feeling his way as the shadows were deep and the area he could see was indistinct. Striking a match, which blinded them briefly, he lifted the chimney and lit the wick. "That's better." Picking up the lamp they headed into the kitchen where they lit a second, followed by the one in the bathroom that sat in the tub. Returning to the living room he set the lamp back on top of the wood stove while Jessie grabbed the double barreled shotgun and set it on the floor between them. They heard the dogs still whining and both had retreated under the house. Jessie and Bill looked at each other as they heard the complaint of the hinges for the backdoor as it was being opened. With some trepidation they got up with both heading into the kitchen which led through a set of interior French doors and out to the backdoor and continued to listen. With it as dark as it was since there was no lamp in the room where the backdoor entered the house they both stood with Jessie carrying the shotgun. They looked at each other and then they reached the French doors when they heard the backdoor close and then they waited . . .

***

While this was happening to the two brothers, the girlfriends had contacted each other and had decided to come up on Saturday and spend time with the brothers – figuring that it would one of the few opportunities for them. Both were in a very serious relationship and knew they would eventually marry the brothers. It was just a matter of when the question would be asked. For now even though it had been somewhat frustrating for the two of them because of the lack of quality time they felt that maybe this weekend they could make up for some of that lost time.

So on Saturday morning they met for breakfast at a local Denney's restaurant for breakfast and then drove out towards where the brothers lived. They were excitedly discussing how their weekend would go when they found the brothers' car broken down on the dirt road. That brought a quick silence and a feeling that something was very wrong. They stopped and checked it out and found it locked and saw a large puddle of something red on the ground. "I hope that's not blood." Leah stated.

But when they got close to it they could see and smell that it had to be something from the car. Since neither was very knowledgeable about the mechanics of a car they assumed this was the reason for the breakdown. But it was mid-morning, so where were the brothers. They would have expected them to be here at the car. Now with some fear in their hearts they continued onto the gate, which was closed and locked. When they got out at the gate they were able to see the brothers' footprints continuing past. "At least it seems they made it home," Jill said.

Both had keys and since Leah was driving Jill unlocked, and then opened the gate while Leah drove through. Once through they locked it again and then drove on down to the property, which sat below the gate. Once there things appeared to be almost normal . . . too normal. But then they realized that they hadn't heard either of the two dogs, and the place seemed vacant and quiet, almost too quiet. Now alarmed they got out and went to the door and knocked but got no answer. So before trying the door they thought let's walk around the house and see if Bill and Jessie might either be in the shop or out back . . . *still no dogs and no sign of them.* What was going on?

Even though they could see the brothers' tracks leading up to the door, and from this evidence, they should be here, yet, the place appeared to be vacant, abandoned. Calling out their names the only sound they heard was the crows that were flying around. *Silence . . . nothing but silence.* What had happened here? As they came around the corner of the house both jumped as they scared a cat that arched its back hissed at them and then took off. Catching her breath Jill said, "My heart's really going. That cat scared the heck right out me."

"You're not alone on that one. Give me a second here to catch my breath." Then looking around she asked, "Where are they? This just doesn't make any sense." Then looking down towards the shop she saw the door was open, and then said, "Ah, I bet they're in the shop. Look the door is open."

Relieved they both headed for the shop, but upon entering found it as vacant as everything else that they had investigated so far. Coming out Leah thought, *I didn't try the lights. Maybe we missed something.* Turning before exiting she tried the light switch and when she turned it on nothing happened. "Looks like there's no power here, I wonder if it's just here or it is the same at the house."

"I don't know, but this is scaring me. I mean really scaring me. Where are they?" The two girls then headed back to the house and continued their interrupted walk around it. Once on the back side where barbecues were held during the summer months, they found the door into the covered patio also open and damaged. Standing there and staring, this mystery was becoming stranger by the minute. "Do you thing we should go in?" Leah asked.

Shaking her head and undecided Jill remained silent for a moment. "I don't know, but if they're inside and hurt, well, we can't help them out here." Eventually their need to know overcame their fear and they decided to go ahead and enter. Once inside briefly waiting until their eyes adjusted to the dim light, both stood frozen in their tracks. Before them used to be the French doors that allowed one to enter the house proper, but they were gone . . . totally destroyed, shattered. What could have done this type of damage?

They knew that once one went through those broken doors you entered into the kitchen, and off to the far end of the kitchen was the living room, which then led to the front door. As they went through these broken doors the next thing they noticed and smelled was blood on the floor – not a small amount either. It definitely had a strong bad odor to it. Gingerly skirting the mess they cautiously entered the living room. On the floor, there at the entrance to the kitchen, they saw a double-barreled shotgun lying there.

Jill picked it up and then opened it, and pulled out the spent cartridges. "Look Leah, both barrels have been fired! My guess is that whatever broke down those doors received both barrels. But where are Bill and Jessie? Again, what happened here . . . I think we had better get out of here and contact the sheriff's department, what do you think?" At this point the mystery kept growing – little evidence and less chance of finding out what had happened last night.

"I agree, and I've been checking and there's no signal for my cell phone, which is what usually happens, so the only way we can make a call is go back out. At first I thought maybe one of us should stay in case they show back up, but upon thinking about it I don't think I want to be left here alone. And I think it would probably be the same for you. Shall we go then?"

They both headed for the front door, glad a decision had been made, but uneasy not knowing what had happened. As they opened the front door to leave both screamed. Not expecting anyone they ran into Bill and Jessie, as the brothers were about to enter the house. Unbelieving the girls stood there seeing the two of them, the two girls looked at each other then at them and asked at the same time, "What happened?"

Bill, holding a shovel, looked at Jessie shrugged and said, "It's a long story and one that is hard for us to believe, but the proof is right here, well it was until we buried it. Anyway it all started when we broke down . . .

Dust

Author's Notes

I have to admit that I do have a love for deserts. Still it is the one place that cannot be taken lightly. Yet, for many it is a place of recreation. Camping, hiking, and off-roading are quite common. And personally I've done all three that I just mentioned. Where I lived at the time, the coast, mountains, and desert all were an easy commute. So if one was so inclined then whatever outdoor adventure one wanted to enjoy, one could.

This short story is about such a group of friends who over the years, before they had families, to the present where they do, have made treks to the dunes with their ATV's and spent many an enjoyable weekend burning off the stress of work and family. It is generally primitive as there are no established campgrounds, and you must bring everything you need, and of course after the weekend haul your trash back with you.

Yet, for one this weekend will not be what he expects. Again, I had a number of images in my mind before writing this short story. And with personal experience I know the subject, the areas, and the enjoyment. Still by being this far out from anything it can turn tragic in a moment. People have died from accidents, and because of the distance many times it's because of the time necessary to reach the scene of the accident and return to the closest medical facilities.

Oh, just as a side note here, in one of the deserts that I frequented one of the scenes from Star Wars was filmed. I'll leave it to you to figure out which movie and scene.

Dust

He had to admit that overall it would be a great weekend. It was one of those that had been planned for a long time. His wife and children were heading to her mother's home to spend some quality time, and he and his friends had a desert outing planned. Yeah, a weekend of camaraderie, and time with his friends that he had known, well most of his life. It really had been a while and those sand dunes had been calling all of them for some time. And now the Siren's call was too strong to ignore. And while on many of these weekend outings the families would be with them, all enjoying each other's company, this time it would only be the guys. It was kind of like it had been in the past, when they would spend numerous weekends out, doing this very thing – back when they all were single.

They met Friday night, and he felt the energy and anticipation in all of them as they joked and horsed around while waiting for the last of their old group to arrive. (Well, to be honest, an additional couple of friends would join them on Saturday.) Ken was always one who said he'd be somewhere at a certain time, but you could guarantee that it would always be later. It just seemed to be the way he was and it hadn't changed over time. When he finally arrived they all grabbed a fountain drink, and headed out. By the time they reached where they were planning to camp it would probably be pushing midnight – but so what. After all, it was just the six of them, and they knew that there would be the members of their clique that would join them early Saturday. This would round out the old group that still remained in the area. Others, as time and demands usually did, had moved out of the area, and the only contacts with them were by phone, email, and texts. After all, life had a tendency to get in the way. In fact they were down to only a couple of times a year that they could do this themselves.

Once outside of the city, the lights faded as did the traffic. And soon all of them were on that 2-lane blacktop that would pass by the dunes. On this night there was a full moon and the road was empty of traffic from the opposite direction. The full moon made the desert seem almost magical and alive. He knew that others were heading to the same area, but because of the different times that they left there never were many on these desert roads. A couple of his friends liked to take their trucks and drive down the road on the wrong side of the road just to be a little crazy. He always smiled, but at the same time shook his head at the sheer stupidity of it. The problem was there were dips in this road that could hide an approaching vehicle and ruin the weekend for all of them. Fortunately they had been lucky in the past, and there hadn't been an accident, but that didn't mean that there never would be.

Eventually they pulled off the roadway onto the wash-boarded dirt surface that passed as a road, shaking their teeth, and rattling the vehicles, forcing them to slow to a crawl. With the moonlight the dunes stood out in eerie silent beauty, and soon with the known landmarks and the many campfires from other camps, they parked at their favorite campsite – nothing official of course. Getting out of their trucks and RV's, all of them stretched and walked out the kinks from being behind the wheel for the few hours that the drive had taken. Tonight they would set up camp, and in the morning unload the 4-wheelers or ATV's to begin their weekend of riding the dunes. The workweek was behind them, and for a short time they could forget all of the responsibilities that life laid upon them, have fun, and remember and talk about it all that following night around their campfire. All of them could feel the pressures of life rolling off of them and with smiles looked around and at each other with great anticipation. The morning would come soon enough.

* * *

It had been a crazy Saturday as they spent most of the day running the dunes in their ATV's and having a great time. (Yes their late arriving friends had come into camp somewhere near midmorning.) They would come in to refuel both the ATV's and themselves, taking breaks now and then, until the urge to get back out would finally overwhelm them, and as if of one mind they'd head for their machines and in a flash of noise and dust be off once again. And as the sun began to set, they reluctantly returned to their camp. And as they began to relax, all of them felt the weariness in their bodies, but at the same time seemed refreshed. Looking around he saw the smiles and distant stares from his old friends of a lifetime.

And after a shared meal and a bit of beer, the camp became quiet as the food added its effect to them individually, and slowly as the night moved on, they drifted off to their sleeping bags, tents, camper shells, and RV's, while their minds drifted off thinking about the last rides they would be doing in the morning before loading their machines, sorry to see it end, and then making the trip back home, and back to reality.

He had to admit that he loved these brief getaways with his friends, and wished they could be longer. But family, the job, and staying ahead of the creditors wouldn't allow this to happen too often . . . Yet when he awakened on Sunday morning something felt different. He didn't know just what, but it did. His truck had a camper shell on it and he had spent the night there. When he and his family came out here for those group and family outings the shell was replaced with a cab-over camper making it easier on the family. But he never needed it for himself – at least for now. He knew, from observation, that later the comfort of that camper would be something he would look forward to, but not now.

Anyway these were the thoughts that were going through his mind at the time he crawled out. As expected, the camp and surrounding area was quiet. The sun was just barely beginning its climb from behind the dunes and the desert morning air was chilled – chilled enough that he reached back into the camper shell and grabbed a jacket. Quickly he went to the fire ring and built a fire. Later it would be unneeded, but for now the heat would be nice. After a few minutes he had the fire going and from there went over and got water on for coffee. They all would need it. Knowing the routine, the rest would all eventually crawl out, get some coffee, eat breakfast, pack up, other than what would be needed for the ATV's, and head out for that final ride. Then they would put the machines back on the trailers, and begin the trip back home, and once back put everything away until next time. Yes, once the camp was broken, all would be lost in their own thoughts as they began that trek that said their time was done, with only the memories of their time out here together remaining within their minds.

That had been his thoughts at the time. But as the morning continued to move, the silence of the area never changed. The normal sounds from the surrounding camps never manifested, and none of the others he had ridden with the day before emerged. *What's going on? This has to be a joke and any minute the guys will show themselves and laugh.* But it didn't happen. He could feel the breezes coming off the dunes, and slowly as the morning got later, began to show a small amount of heat. And the silence around him remained. Finally he checked out the other vehicles, and all of them were empty. The tents that a couple of his friends were using showed the same results. Looking around he thought that his friends had to be hiding and watching him and probably laughing silently at his puzzlement. But looking around there was no place to hide – none at all. Maybe they went far enough out that they were hiding in the dunes, but there wasn't any proof of that. So where were they?

Truthfully, he had to admit, none of this made any sense at all. After all, his friends' vehicles were still parked where each one of them had left them. And he could see the equipment left out for that last run of the day – the ATV's sitting showing the dust of the rides from the previous day, and the sun shining off the chrome creating a sparkling reflection that would temporarily blind one from its intensity. He quickly walked to each vehicle, each RV, knocked on the doors, and with no answer tried the handles. None of them were locked and cautiously he entered not knowing what he would find. Yet in each case the units, the camper shells, the tents, all of them were empty. Again, this didn't make any sense at all. He couldn't have imagined yesterday. He had to admit that he felt the soreness in his body from the rides, which brought a smile to him. In the years past – too many really – they had made this trip so often that the soreness he was feeling now never happened.

Now what? He asked himself, but had no ready answers, or a direction at this moment. He went to his own pickup and sat behind the wheel resting his arms on it trying to think this through. After all, weren't there seven others here last night, did they not all enjoy a quiet evening after a full day of fun and riding, and finally, if he was alone, how did all these vehicles and ATV's get here? *And the silence continued.* Once again he realized that it wasn't just their camp, but all the surrounding camps. He couldn't hear the voices drifting with the wind, as it generally happened. And where was the sound of that lone vehicle starting and idling, or the sounds of other ATV's and off-road vehicles being started, loaded, or being prepared as they usually were, for that final ride of the day. None of this was happening, none of it at all . . . Again, just that deafening silence.

Getting out of his truck he heard the sound of his boots crunching on the rock and sand and when he closed his door it sounded much too loud in the surrounding silence. The winds were beginning to pick up and with them the sounds that they produced. At times sounding like a low moaning, and whistling. Followed by the sands in the dunes moving creating their own unique sounds, but that was all. He might as well have been in this world all alone, which he had to admit, was impossible. Taking a deep breath he took one more circuit around their camp, double checked every vehicle, every tent, counting all the equipment that was here, and found, as he had earlier, that everything was here. Nothing missing, all accounted for, so no one had driven off into either the sunset or sunrise. Again, what's happening? He had to admit he didn't have a clue.

Standing there and undecided as to what to do next, he leaned against his truck with his legs crossed trying to think this whole situation through. Then he smiled as a thought crossed his mind. Maybe, just maybe he was asleep and all of this was a dream – a powerful one for sure, but a dream. After all, what other explanation made any sense – none that he could think of at this moment. *So, if this is a dream, how do I wake myself up?* Yet, when he looked around it seemed too real. *But, weren't dreams that way?* He asked himself. When one was in a dream everything within that dream seemed to be real, and it would only be when one awakened that the truth would be revealed.

Now he found that he was second guessing himself. Was what he was experiencing a dream or not? And if it is a dream, how did one awaken from it? Yet, once again, what he was experiencing seemed too real to be a dream. Shaking his head, he had to admit he was going in circles. Looking up since he'd been looking down as he thought this through, he could see that the morning was advancing. Coming to a decision he decided to ride his ATV around the area to the other camps that were close by and see if there were people there. Since, in his mind, he felt that this still could be an elaborate joke, and if there were others around, this would confirm it. With the decision made he strode purposely to his ATV climbed aboard and started it. Again, like the door of his truck when he closed it earlier, the sound of the ATV starting seemed much too loud.

After making the decision to head out and check other camps he found himself undecided. He sat astride his ATV and let it idle. If one wasn't invited into another camp, one stayed away. It was an unwritten courtesy that all of them practiced. Again, with camping being the way it was, it was next to impossible to lock everything up. Finally coming to a decision once again, he shrugged and headed out going slowly so that he could look as he putted around. He figured that he could approach one of the other camps and yell out to the occupants and get permission to come in. And if nobody seemed to be around, drive up close enough that he could check it out, but not so close as to be intruding.

The first camp he checked out wasn't that far from their camp, and like their own camp, it appeared to be vacant. Vehicles were parked, and partially packed up for the return trip, but nothing else. As he toured the rest of the camps close by, the results were all the same. *What's going on?* He found that he was beginning to have doubts and fears. This was too crazy. With what he was discovering he kept coming back to his dream conclusion, but it didn't really fit. Again he asked himself, "Now what?"

With the sun making its steady climb into the sky,

time was becoming a factor. If he was to reach home when he needed he had to be on the road, well, now. But he didn't want to leave any of his friends behind, or leave anything unattended as it seemed to be presently. Still what could he do about it – nothing really. If no one was around then everything here should be safe, but would it be? And by leaving, would he be abandoning his friends? He had no answers, and with no answers forthcoming he loaded his ATV back on his trailer, tied it down, checked and rechecked his equipment, climbed into his truck and once again sat there undecided.

Leaning on the steering wheel he took a deep breath, took one last look around, reluctantly started his truck, and slowly left the camp area, stopping a number of times and almost turning around and going back to the camp. He knew that once he was back on that blacktop road that he would be worrying all the way back home.

* * *

He remembered, as he drove down that blacktop road, to look out into the areas where others rode. There were always those who either had more time off, or left later, allowing all of them, as they drove away, one last look at the lucky ones that would still be out riding. Yet, there was nothing, other than the *dust* being blown about by the increasing desert winds. This was too weird, and it sent chills up and down his spine. Then he glanced at the passenger seat, since he had been looking out to his left, and there appeared to be a stranger sitting there, who turned and smiled. It startled him so much that he lost control of his truck.

Fighting hard to bring it back under control, and keep it on his side of the road, he was finally successful. He knew if there had been oncoming traffic he was sure he would have hit at least one of them – not good. Once he had both his beating heart and breath under control he turned to ask this stranger who he was. But, the seat was empty – had he imagined it? Well, it kind of added to his dream theory. Yet, once again, if this was a wild dream, why hadn't he awakened?

With no answers forthcoming, he took a deep breath, concentrated on his driving, and headed down that straight and empty desert road. He knew that once he crested the mountains that bordered the desert they would normally pull into a gas station combination coffee shop, fill their vehicles and themselves, and know that once finished that basically the weekend was over, and this would be the final time that they would be together. Once they left the coffee shop it would be as individuals heading to their personal homes, followed by the cleanup of their equipment, and the preparation to return to their jobs the next day. But that was still at least an hour or more away. He still worried that he had abandoned his friends back at the camp, but what choice did he have?

Other than what he figured had to be his imagination, with someone sitting in the passenger seat, and all the weirdness that seemed be happening, something was still bothering him and he couldn't quite figure it out. He was listening to a CD since radio reception was spotty at the best in the area, and had it on loud enough to override the humming of the tires on the road. It was one of his favorite groups from the time of his youth and he found himself singing along with a few of his favorite songs. Yet, he kept feeling a nervousness rising as his sixth sense kept trying to tell him something. Something felt wrong, not that everything that had transpired this day hadn't, but this was pointing to something else – in another direction.

When they normally returned home they would head back a different way than the way they headed out. By going south they would pick up a major freeway, making travel easier, and, of course, make that final stop to refuel. Nothing like this existed on the route out. He was now on that freeway heading up the steep grade and suddenly realized that he hadn't heard the Jake-brakes or exhaust-brakes of the tractor-trailers heading down that same grade leaving the mountains and heading towards the desert floor. Nor had he seen any heading down the grade or had he passed any slowly making their way up the same grade. It was a six percent grade for heaven sake. Then it struck him that not only was there no trucks, but there were no cars, nor anything else for that matter. He was it, period. This really made no sense since this was one of the few routes across the desert, and one that all the truckers used – let alone anybody else just passing through.

It was what his mind had been trying to tell him. Not only had he awoke to an empty camp and surrounding area, but there was no one on the roads either. *Once again, what is going on?* There was a rest area on this route so he quickly pulled in. He needed to get out and stretch, use the facilities, and try his cell phone. Sometimes one would get lucky from this spot and actually make a call. But consistent with all that had been happening to this point, luck was against him. And no matter where he walked, in the area, the phone came back with "no service". Finally giving up he got back into his truck and once again headed out on an empty silent freeway and to what future he had no idea. And at this point he wasn't sure if he truly wanted to know anyway, but knew that he couldn't remain here. Besides it wouldn't be long until he would be at their final stop and he was sure that he would get his answers there – at least one could hope. This couldn't continue, could it?

***

It was pushing one thirty in the afternoon when he pulled off the freeway towards the gas station to fill up the truck and himself. He found that he was starving, since he had forgotten to eat anything that morning back at the camp. He was hoping, since where this stop was located was on the edge of a small rural community, that there would be others doing the same thing. So he expected to find the usual crowd that hung out here and at the coffee shop – many from that rural community. In fact it would be a relief to actually see some familiar strangers instead of nobody. So dropping from the speeds of the freeway to that of a rural road he felt like he was crawling. Taking a deep breath he pulled into the gas station, and other that a flock of birds that he flushed, the station gave the appearance of being just as vacant as the camp and the roads.

He pulled up to a pump, sat there quietly while the truck idled and put his head on the steering wheel, closing his eyes, and feeling the weariness in his mind and body. This stop was something that they all looked forward to. It represented the end to an enjoyable weekend, and the last chance before returning to reality – but not this time. Instead of an anticipation of friendship and togetherness, he felt dread. How else should he feel? And where is everybody?

Finally he got out and stretched. The winds were whipping and held some heat, which was no surprise, since this town sat on the edge of the mountains overlooking the desert. Looking around he saw the scrub brush that covered the hillsides moving with the wind, and smell of the hot sage as those same winds brought the scents to him. He felt the heat coming up from the pavement and it was hot enough that the bottoms of his shoes were letting his feet know that he had better move. He smiled at all the sensations and feelings coming back to him. At least he felt that he was alive, and not crazy. Well, he hoped not anyway. Still with the silence and nothing moving, other than the winds, and what they were blowing around, he couldn't be sure.

Walking inside he found the station unattended, and with the rest of the day it was almost expected. At least he could self-serve. He returned and pumped the gas, at least enough to get him home. Gas was a bit expensive here, but there was little that one could do about it since its location was such that it was a necessary stop. He took the receipt from the pump, got back into the truck and wrote down the mileage, started the truck and drove over to the vacant parking lot of the coffee shop. Getting out he went to the door to enter and to his disappointment found the doors were locked. Putting his face to the glass doors he looked inside the shadowed space and nothing was moving at all, and no lights were on. It might as well have been an abandoned town and a dead world.

Walking back over to the gas station, at least here he could get something to eat as they had refrigerated cases that included sandwiches and such for those in a hurry. Again, in a quandary, he picked up some food, filled a fountain drink, went to the empty counter, and really had no idea what to do at this point. He couldn't very well pay for what he had in his hands. So after thinking about it he decided that he would leave a note explaining what he took, and that he would settle with them later. It took a while to locate something to write on, and he wasn't sure if he wanted to leave it where anybody could find it. Finally after looking around a bit he settled on a place behind the counter where other papers seemed to be stored, headed back outside, walked back to his truck, opening both doors, sat there and ate his lunch hoping somebody, anybody would show up. But no one did – only the silence, the heat and the blowing winds. Still, he wondered how that fresh food got there in the cases. It didn't just magically appear. But he had no answers for this inconsistency.

* * *

It took a couple of hours to get home and it was pushing between four and five PM when he arrived. He backed the truck into the driveway, and noticed that his wife and children hadn't returned yet. At least it would give him time to get everything back to where it belonged, and probably be able to take a shower before the chaos began. It was always that way; a silent quiet house until the children arrived and then chaos, noise, and energy. Well, he had to admit that for now the quiet was welcome. Shower time, time to get all that dirt off, and let the hot water refresh him so he could face his family's arrival. He suspected that they would be bringing home pizza so he didn't start anything for dinner, and decided to wait until after the shower before calling Sue to let her know that all was well with him. That stopped him for a moment, was it well with him? He thought so, but this day had been much too weird for his taste. And while he didn't look about too much once he got home he suspected that there was no one around the neighborhood – but again that didn't make any sense.

Once out of the shower he called Sue on her cell phone, but there was no answer. Well, she might be on the road, and if so wouldn't answer. So he decided to call Sue's mom and dad, but the results were the same – no answer and just the answering machine asking him to leave a message. Worried now, he didn't know what to do. Sue's family wasn't close so he couldn't just jump in his truck and drive there. He went outside, even though he knew it was too early for her to be back, and watched the road in the direction she would be approaching – nothing. Nothing but worry that is.

After a few hours had passed, he felt the weariness dragging at him. And still no answers from anybody he had called and no sounds in the neighborhood either. He thought about calling the police, but what could he tell them? Nobody had committed a crime, and there had been no accidents, everything was quiet, so for now he resisted the urge. He suddenly realized that deep in his subconscious there had been a slight and steady beep happening – one so subtle that it had taken him until now to realize that it was there – could it be the alarm? Could all of this really be a dream? Finally giving up he went to bed worried sick over what was transpiring, but with nothing to show him that there really was something going on, other than with him. He was at a loss, and was at a loss at what he could do personally to change any of this. Maybe it was a dream and what he was hearing was the alarm, but it really hadn't penetrated yet.

Exhaustion took him and he awoke slowly that next morning with the sun in his eyes. It took him back to his youth as he saw the *dust* dancing in the rays of sunlight. He remembered making stories of that floating *dust*, and that brought a smile to him. Taking a deep breath, he moved over slightly, rolled over, and with that beeping getting stronger in his mind, but still barely heard, he drifted off to sleep once more.

Suddenly that beeping became important, critical really, and he didn't know why. Yet, once again, it might be that alarm that was always unwelcome. But he felt a weariness that made it almost impossible to reach out and shut that darn thing off. He expected Sue to climb over him and hit it for him since he was so slow, but it didn't happen. But then again, she hadn't been there last night. Was the nightmare going to continue? He took a deep breath as he began to really wake up. He slowly opened his eyes, and found that instead of his own bed he was in a hospital bed. Looking up and then to his right he saw Sue sitting next to his bed looking out the window with a worried tired expression on her face. *What happened? And why am I here? And why is Sue looking so worried?* No answers came to him so he shifted to reach out and touch her only to see her react to his movement and look him right in the eyes followed by a big smile, saying, "You had us worried that you wouldn't make it." She took a deep and tired breath. "You have been in here hovering close to death for at least a week, and nobody, not the doctors, or nurses, knew whether you'd pull through or not. Do you remember anything at all? And I am so glad to see you finally awake – so, so glad." Here she was silent as he could see the emotions playing across her face, and tears of joy forming in her eyes.

Remember anything? A week had gone by? What's she talking about, and why am I here? All of this ran through his mind, but not for long as a heavy weariness lay upon him and he found himself drifting back into a deep sleep. It was two weeks later when he was well on the way to recovery that he learned what had happened. They were heading down the grade that Friday night, heading towards the desert. They were following one of those big rigs and he was directly behind it. They knew that once they reached the desert floor that all of them would pass it and get on with the weekend – but it was not to be.

A rare occurrence occurred, where the big rig blew two tires, which threw it out of control, taking another tire with it. One of the blown tires had disintegrated followed by one of the large chunks crashing into his truck, coming over the hood and shattering the windshield. This caused him to lose control and crash into the careening big rig, which jackknifed and turned over, crushing part of his truck and pinning him inside. It was hours later that they were able to extract him and life-flight him to hospital where he had barely clung to life, with the prognosis of death, and the anticipated weekend never happened. The riding, the *dust*, the camaraderie with his friends, was all in his mind. So all of what he had experienced, in a way, was a dream. But, in the end, he never did figure out who that stranger was who had been in his truck that day as he headed home, and probably never would. And if he thought too hard about it, he might have considered it the turning point, choosing life over death. And maybe, in the scheme of things, with life ahead of him, it wasn't really important after all.

A Thanksgiving to Remember

Author's Notes

While this story is fictitious, the events stated in this short story happened. In fact it happened to me, and my family to include my parents, and one of my brothers and his family. The wildfire spoken of in this short story is named Cedar, and the year was 2003, the month October, with the wildfire destroying all the homes on the property late in that month.

This is one of two short stories reflecting that event. The second is titled, Fire on the Mountain, which has already been read since it is earlier in this novel of short stories. I must admit that personally I can still see images in my mind of that time. There is an old phrase that is much overused, but is probably one that is true. "Walk a mile in my shoes." Why, you may ask, what I've learned in life is that until you have followed in the path of another you can never fully appreciate or understand.

In my youth I was a wildland firefighter having fought a number of large fires. These fires, which burned thousands of acres, didn't wait around to do this. So when I write about wildfires I do know what I'm writing is fact. Just a little factoid, in the novel Discovery, book two of the Discovery Trilogy, a wildfire plays a role in the overall story.

In this short story we follow only the one family as

they face this day, and here in the United States, a day of thanksgiving. The wildfire destroyed the homes at the end of October, and Thanksgiving was about one month later. Still with the conditions, the loss, the tragedies, they still felt like they had valid reasons to be thankful. And with this intro it's onto the short story, A Thanksgiving to Remember.

A Thanksgiving to Remember

The winds whipped out of the northeast with a vengeance. Unfortunately it was a very cold wind, and dry. It picked up the ash and blew it around in black clouds covering them in soot and ash. If they could look into a mirror they would have sworn that they were coal miners with faces, and any exposed skin black. Large whirlwinds picked up more of the ash and danced across the barren, burned, and blackened landscape creating ghostly monsters dancing to their own music. The tents that they were living in were laid flat not being able to stand against the furiousness of the winds and their more powerful gusts. Then the pegs ripped out of the ground whipping the ropes into the air, followed by the shredding of the same tents. It really appeared that nature in her fury wanted to destroy anything that still remained – anything manmade. All the family could do was hold on and hope that soon these winds would diminish in intensity and leave them alone.

The only consolation that any of them had was the knowledge that they were not alone – not that they wished their plight on others. When the fires had ripped through the area there had been little warning and almost no time to escape. All they owned presently was what they were able to get into their cars before fleeing. The rest was abandoned and what had been abandoned was a total loss. The fires had been intense, pushed by similar winds which they were facing now, but this fire had been different from others from the past. Oh yes so much different. After all, it wasn't uncommon for these winds to push wildfires such as these, but this one burned into these winds. Ah, one would think, if that was so, then it should have been easy to control, easy to extinguish, after all that meant that this fire had to fight for every foot. But alas it was not so. It burned with an intensity that defied belief, and with a speed completely unexpected – again into the winds of all things. In the end the ones *in the know* stated that this was a topography and fuel driven fire. What the winds had provided was the spark, the low humidity, a way to spread the fire at the beginning. Once on the move it became a monster with a mind of its own, going where it pleased, not stopping and ignoring anything or anyone.

At first this fire was to the north of their location, far away, and while worrisome did not appear, in the beginning, as one that would have any effect on them. *After all, the winds would push it away from their location, and all that would be necessary was to monitor it.* Yet it hadn't remained to north of them and had traveled south against those winds after being pushed west. Once west of their location it consumed everything in its path burning directly and rapidly into those strong winds. They had remained up late that previous night watching with disbelief as the mountain to the west of where they lived was consumed. With the rising sun all that could be seen in the west was a heavy dark boiling smoke cloud rising into the sky. This smoke cloud, running from the southwest to the northwest, with a sharp defined break between the hot boiling smoke being produced by the fire, and the clear blue skies, leaving none to doubt what was happening beneath that veil. The summer had been long and hot with no moisture, the winter before producing very little rain, leaving them in a heavy drought. The irony being this; the day the wild fire ended it *rained*.

Yes it had rained a cold rain which lasted a couple of days. Rusting the exposed burned metal left from the fires that had consumed the wood and other materials. The fire had been so hot that a barbeque was consumed leaving a skeleton of what it once was. But at least the rains were light. With nothing to hold the soils it could have resulted in another disaster following on the heels of the one caused by the fires. There easily could have been mudslides and flash flooding, adding to the misery and loss. So for this small miracle they were thankful. Yet where did one go from here? Their location had been remote and insurance impossible to get. So yes the question that lay before them was just that; where did they go from here? Yet, right at this moment it was the winds that were once again on their minds. It was Thanksgiving Day, and obviously they would not be celebrating it here. Thankfully other family members lived outside the zone of destruction and they were to head there instead – a small respite, a chance to reflect. With a future dark and unknown, and a past that had made them homeless, made them refugees in their own land, but maybe, just maybe, from this would be lessons of life. For many in this world were as such, and many families in this county, like theirs, had no place to live, no place to stay, and no real answers.

Yet today was a celebration of life, of being thankful for what they had, what they had endured, what they had survived – others hadn't been as fortunate. So even with all that had transpired, all that had been lost, the hard times that they had faced, and would continue to face, they still had much to be thankful for. Things such as each other, and the support of family, the reaching out of strangers for the needs that existed, and most of all with all this destruction, the loss of personal items, family heirlooms, their home, in the end it was just stuff. No one died, not one was injured, and while the future was unknown, and full of unknown problems, at this time, at this very moment, it was enough.

Returning Home

Author's Notes

Many times before beginning a short story I see a situation, or ask myself, "What if?" Then for a period of time the idea sits in the back of my mind and cooks while the everyday stuff of life continues on. For most of the stories, as I've stated, it is the imagery that I see that begins the written word. And sometimes it is the combination of both. And this is one of these.

While I had been writing stories for Christmas I hadn't created any for Thanksgiving, which is the third Thursday of November here in the US. So I consciously thought about writing one. As I let my mind work on this slowly I saw the imagery and direction this short story was to take. Again, like my Christmas short stories, this one is Christian based.

Many times, once we are grown, life gets into the way of things we hold dear. You know things such as family gatherings, which, if one wants to be honest, Thanksgiving perfectly represents. And for many this is one of the few times where it can happen. Yet for others, as much as they might desire to come together with family, life gets in the way.

And this is the direction this short story takes. Our protagonist is returning home for the first time in too many years. And as he walks the dirt road of his youth memories flood back to him. And these memories push him onward. And now onto the short story: Returning Home.

Returning Home

It was a cold autumn evening, dusk was just settling in on the land as he wrapped his thin well-worn coat around him. The coat as well as the clothes he wore had seen better days. Still he had to admit to himself that so had he. Still there was a smile on his face because he was returning home after all these years. Years that seemed to drift off into a past that was unremembered and unwanted. He shivered briefly when the breeze found a way past the patched jacket and touched his skin. If he had a mirror he would have seen an old man with his personal history written in every wrinkle, every line of his face. His face, and he had to admit most of his body, showed signs of a hard life, one spent mostly outdoors, mostly away the centers of what could be called civilization, never having enough of anything.

Looking ahead he could see the winding dirt road that would bring him back to his beginnings, and what had transpired since he had left now meant nothing. In many ways he figured that like so many he had wasted his life, and somehow time just had gotten away from him. When he thought about this too deeply it led to a deep depression, a hurt that was hard to find a way out or to get away from. So he tried not to press too hard in that direction, but just let his destination be his happiness for now. What happened later was in the future and he knew from experience that no one controlled the future, least of all him. Sighing and taking a deep breath that he let out slowly he looked at that final hill. That one that always said that home was close, but at the same time required effort to conquer.

I guess if I stand right here I'll never make it back, he thought. Then smiling once again he said, "Time's a wastin'", and began that final climb that would lead to the top of a hill through an old broken gate, leading down the other side, and then into the place where the house sat, a place where he had once called home. Dusk was upon him and he needed to hurry if he was to be there before it became dark. But what did it matter? After all he had walked this way too many times to even count and he could do it in his sleep, or in the darkness of a moonless night. There was a dampness on the land that he could smell and feel, a muskiness that spoke of fallen leaves, and of newly turned soil, which flooded his mind with memories of his childhood – making him smile once more as these memories flooded his mind. It really did seem like it was only yesterday and he was just returning home from school, anticipating a snack when he got there, and at the same time dreading the chores that always waited.

He stopped, once through that broken gate, as memories once again flooded his mind. This always had been a place to pause, to look out over the vastness that fell away from here. He remembered that on those clear days and nights you could look down upon the cities that were far to the west, and on those clear days all the way to the coast. At night, between the stars and the city lights, all twinkling, their lights magical in the distance, leaving one intrigued as to what was there, making the imagination soar. He breathed in the fresh damp clear air, although if his eyesight wasn't failing him, it appeared that the fog was beginning to creep in. This brought a flood of new memories as he remembered the times that the fog would lay just below them leaving an ocean of white that made it appear that they were on the coast, next to an ocean, with the beach within walking distance. Then as the sun heated the fog it would lift and cover them in its grayness for a short period of time until that sun would burn it off leaving a clear warm day ahead. With that smile still on his face he shook his head, *so many good memories*, he thought, *again where has the time gone, and with it all those passing years?* Yes those passing years that seemed to drift off into nothingness, beyond the reach of his memory.

He stayed long enough to catch his breath because that still was a heavy climb that hadn't gotten any easier with those passing years. And as he cooled from his exertions he decided that he had better get moving once again. He really didn't like getting cold. The road before him twisted slightly to the right before heading steeply downhill. Once past this portion he knew that it turned to the right and eventually turned again to the left as it wound its way to his destination. And just before that right turn over half way down this hill sat a sunken boulder that didn't allow anything to grow. It was a place known to the family as dead man's curve, even though it had never lived up to its name. Again he stopped here because from here he could see the house partially hidden below and he saw that ol' porch light giving light to the darkness that surrounded it – a beacon in the night. Again he stopped as those memories came flooding back. *Why has it taken so long to return?* Still he knew that it was nostalgia and those romantic ideas that were flooding his mind, hiding the other side. Yet, here he stood once again and was almost home, just standing for a short time enjoying those flashes of the past. Still, he had to admit that they were good memories – great memories really.

Finally, as he took a deep breath of the cool country air, he continued his hike down into the yard where he heard the dogs barking. There always had been dogs and he saw that this hadn't changed. He could hear the rattle of their chains. As it always had been, they were chained for the night so that they couldn't roam the hills. In the yard he viewed the many parked cars speaking to him that all the family had gathered and he suspected that he would be the last one to arrive. And sure enough as he came closer to the house the door opened and one of his siblings stood there smiling at him and beckoning him to come inside and join them for which he happily did. Going from the cool damp outside air to a warm inside made him feel overly warm. But he knew that shortly he would adjust and the outside would seem much too cold. He smelled the delicious smells of the turkey in the oven, the sights of the pies, yams, potatoes, and so many other delectable temptations. Yes, it did appear that this would be as it had been in the past – a time of Thanksgiving, a time of family, and a time of happy memories.

There were no young children since all of them, his siblings and he, were older. This last gathering was only for the children of their parents who had passed away many years before. It probably was the last time that all of them would be together and this made it even more special – so much more precious. Time and life had a way of making such gatherings nearly impossible and it had been too many years since they were able to gather this way. His brothers and sisters were there. After all they had been a large family and one that had always been close. But time and life had gotten in the way and it was rare, such a gathering as this. They sat and reminisced about their lives here, bringing much laughter, and a few tears as story after story passed between them bringing all of them back to those times when this was home. Finally it was time to eat and to give a prayer of thanks to God for allowing this to take place and for the guidance and protection that he had provided over their lives.

Even here the conversations never died as all were brought up to date with what had been happening in each other's lives. He felt warm and comfortable enjoying every moment because it would be all that he had. For even joyful gatherings like this had a beginning, and as life, had an ending. And as full as everybody was from the meal there was still pie and coffee and more conversation, with much companionship and joy. Eventually as the food began to take effect the conversation slowly died as all relaxed overly full and almost uncomfortable. Such was a Thanksgiving meal. And as the conversation died a stranger walked in from the kitchen signaling him to follow. Curious he got up noticing that the rest of the family wasn't really paying much attention. They probably assumed that he was heading for the bathroom; after all it was in this direction. When he reached the stranger the stranger whispered, "Follow me, I have something important to show you."

Questioning but still curious he followed him out of

the living room through the kitchen, out the double doors, through the dining room which was still stacked with uneaten food and dirty dishes, then outside through the back door. It was chilly as it was fall and darkness had fully fallen. It was at this time that the stranger turned to him saying, I've been sent to fetch you. For it is your time to go home."

Not understanding he said, "But I am home. I'm seeing my family, and my joys are being with them and what they represent."

This stranger looked at him smiling kindly. "Yes this is true but there is so much more than this. And this is not your final home. I'm here to take you there."

"Ah, now I understand. Can I at least say goodbye?"

Again the stranger smiled, "They already know", was all he said.

* * *

It was the day after Thanksgiving and she was sitting down reading a magazine. After all like her children she had the day after off. Her husband was stuck and had to work. It always seemed to be the way. Her two boys were out and exploring as they always liked to do when there was nothing pressing for them to do. They were nine and eleven – prime age for imagination and exploration. They had moved to country five years in the past and she had never regretted the move. Beyond them were abandoned properties where no one had lived in years. The road past their place was impassible to even 4 wheel drive vehicles and the only way one could get back to most of these properties was on foot. Even motorcycles found it close to impassable. With a few accidents it had been marked as hiking only.

She remembered hiking back to some of those properties and had idly wondered about the ones who had lived here back when it had been occupied. But now there were barely trails, and the fields and open spaces almost taken over by the wild grasses and brush that seemed so prevalent. The houses were nothing more than ruins, barely standing, but great places for adventures for her boys. She wanted to be sure that it was safe for them to explore these old houses and once satisfied, with the urging of her husband, relented and allowed them to explore to their heart's content. At this time they were the furthest out and rarely did they see anybody other than ones who were lost who would stop by to get directions. So with the boys out doing their exploring, she was taking advantage of the peace and quiet with none of the normal chaos going on around her. Even the dogs were quiet and lazy. So these rare opportunities were much appreciated.

Suddenly the dogs began excitedly to bark. She recognized the bark as someone they knew but didn't know who it could be. After all she didn't expect the boys back for a couple of hours. Then they came rushing into the house all excited about something. She gave them that look that made them quit running, followed this by asking, "Okay, what's going on here?"

"Mom", her oldest began, "we decided that we wanted to go over the hill and go play in that old house, you know the one that you and dad said we could."

She wasn't sure where this was leading so she said, "Okay, sure . . ."

"Well we were having a great adventure playing like we were retreating from an enemy and that old house would be our fort. We were having so much fun and when we came up to that old house we burst in like we were being chased. But that changed once we got inside." Here he paused.

Sensing that something wasn't right she said quietly, "Continue please."

"Ah, we ran through the, what you and dad called the living room, through the old kitchen and then out in that other room. It was there that we found him."

"Found him? Was someone there? Did he bother you?" She asked alarmed. *I told Mike not to let the boys go there by themselves,* she thought.

"No, no, he didn't bother us. He was an old man and he appeared to be sleeping, but when he didn't wake up we figured he had to be dead."

"Are you sure?"

"Ah mom, of course we're sure. We tried to wake him and he didn't move. Then we saw that he was staring at the ceiling and he was cold."

She got up quickly from her comfortable couch and immediately called emergency services which stated that they would be out immediately.

* * *

Later she heard a helicopter pass overhead and assumed that it was emergency services. After a while a unit showed up at her door. A polite young man came to the door and knocked. She let him in and he brought her up to date with what they had found. He had told her that yes the old man was dead and from what they could tell he had died the night before, and no there was no foul play. It appeared he had died of old age. And how he got there they never knew, but from the worn out condition of his clothing they concluded that he was poor and maybe somehow had gotten lost and had took shelter there since last night was cold, fell asleep and never woke up. It surely was a mystery and one that would never have an answer.

* * *

He stood silently in shock; he seemed to be standing on a plain that went into the distance as far as he could see. Before him stood his parents looking younger than he last remembered them who were smiling at him with joy on their faces saying, "We've been waiting for this day when you would join the rest of us, and now we will be together as a family forever, we've missed you, as you were the last."

At first he was confused since he was sure that he had been at that Thanksgiving gathering with all his brothers and sisters. He quickly looked around and indeed saw all of his immediate family smiling and filled with the joy that only such reunions can bring and knowing that they would never be separated again. He understood at that moment that this had been arranged for him and they were waiting in anticipation for his coming home, completing their family as it once had been, and when he looked at his hands he no longer saw ones that were damaged by age and infirmaries, but ones of his youth, and knew that indeed he was home and it was a time of great Thanksgiving.

A Christmas Story

Author's Notes

When I started my blog back in May of 2011 I really hadn't thought about writing a Christmas short story. And with this one I began a tradition where I'd present one each year. So from 2011 through to the publication of this book of short stories in 2018 I wrote a Christmas short story. And in some cases with the feedback from readers I then added a second part – a second or closing chapter so to speak.

I had an image in my mind that was the inspiration behind the story. Yet, before I began to write I had to determine which way the story would go. I felt that there were lots of "feel good" stories out there, and knew from experience that many don't have a good or great Christmas. In fact many end in tragedy. So while these Christmas stories are written with less than great times they aren't necessarily negative.

Here's the image I saw that led to this short story: It is night – a very dark night. It's snowing heavily and the narrow road that the car is traveling is covered in show. On both sides of the road there's heavy vegetation that would probably reach the height of the car. The driver is on his way home to his family. Looking out the windshield I see the falling snow forming patterns in the headlights that can and will distract, pulling one's attention away. I hear the windshield wipers and see the headlights as they attempt to penetrate the falling snow. And with this the story fell into place and became the first of the seven presented here.

Yet, later I felt the need to write part two. Again I saw an image. This image was of his home and family as they awaited his arrival. I saw the house and how the street lay which sat below the picture window looking out over the driveway where he'd park before coming inside. I felt the anticipation and the desire for his arrival. And this became the rest of the story.

A Christmas Story Part One

It was late Christmas Eve; he had been heading home anticipating the warmth and joys that would be at the end of his drive. But it was not to be. The falling snow had mesmerized him and he lost his direction, only for a moment, but it was enough. His car slid through the bushes that lined the side of the road, and his automobile crashed head-on into a tree. He lay there in his broken car, with his broken body, finding it difficult to breathe. Any movement brought great pain, and he could feel the cold creeping in all around him. He knew for a fact, that this would be his last night on earth. He knew that his loved ones would be awaiting his arrival with anticipation, but that wait would be in vain. He would not show tonight. How he wished it would be different, how he hoped that what had transpired would only be a dream, but in his heart, in his soul he knew the truth. He did not know how much more time he had, but knew his time was very short.

As he tried to find a comfortable position in the darkness and cold of his car, he found that any movement at all brought great pain. *Why tonight?* Why on this special night before the celebration of the birth of the Savior had this come to pass? He had no answers, but knew that time was not promised to anyone. He wondered what it would be like to die, and knew that shortly he personally would learn. No one knew where he was, and he was sure that the falling snow would have covered any tracks he would have left. He was utterly alone. He thought of his family that he would be leaving behind, and cried. He could no longer help them or watch his children as they grew.

He closed his eyes briefly and when he opened them he thought that he was hallucinating. As he looked he saw someone sitting in the passenger seat. Taking a painful breath, he closed his eyes once again thinking that when he opened them the seat would be empty. Yet, when he did open his eyes this person was still there. This person then turned to him and smiled. "I am real, and I have been sent by the Lord God Almighty to bring you home. And don't try to talk as I can hear your thoughts. I am here to lessen the pain, and help you. To make you understand that God and his son Christ will continue to watch over your family, and while they will miss you, time will eventually help them. You see, each and every one of you must walk your own road, and when God places problems and situations in front of you, the way that you decide to handle each one determines your direction.

"Remember God has seen every path that you can take in your life, and knows you completely. You accepted his Son as your personal Savior a very long time ago, and you have lived a life that reflects that. It shows in the love for your family, and for your fellow man. So, some of those decisions have led you to this moment in time. The time here is brief, and where you are going will make this appear as nothing more than shadow. So God's gift for you is that you will be with him tonight. And while it will be a sad time for your family, your gift to them tonight is that they will remember you at this time of year, and while the memories are still fresh, these memories will be hard. Yet, you will precede them, and when it is their turn you will welcome them with joy, as they see the Savior with their own eyes. As this dawn is the celebration of the birth of Christ, you will be able to celebrate with them when they come home."

It was a lot to take in, to understand. Still the words he heard were comforting. He smiled as he faded into unconsciousness . . .

He was found late Christmas day when a chance glance located the point where the car had left the road. Another tragedy on Christmas Eve, yet, no one could understand the slight smile on the dead man's face, which his broken body could not explain. He truly appeared to be at peace.

A Christmas Story Part Two

"Mama, where is daddy?" The young daughter asked. It was getting late on Christmas Eve and he should have arrived by now.

Shaking her head and trying to hide the worry and concern that she felt, she said. "I really don't know. The weather is pretty bad out there and it has been snowing for hours." She walked to the lightly frosted windows looking out trying to catch sight of his approaching car, but only saw the patterns that the falling snow created as it passed through the porch and lighted walkway that led to the front door. It warm and cozy in the house, but she felt a chill. *Just where is my husband, my man?* She thought. *He really should have been home hours ago.*

Again shaking her head and looking at the three children, she really had no answers to give them, and did not know what to tell them. Then putting on a brave face she said, "I'm sure it's just the weather that has slowed him down. You know that he is always careful when he drives in these storms. So I'm sure this is what has kept him from us." Then looking around at the room she saw the fire burning in the fireplace and reflected on the comfort it seemed to give. She then looked up at the clock and it said 9:00. *He's hours late.* "Look, children, I'll allow you to stay up another half hour, but if your father doesn't show by then, well, you'll just have to go to bed. And then when he gets here he can come in and tuck all of you in." She found something on TV to entertain them while she left and got her well-used Bible. She feared the worst, but hoped for the best.

Since it was Christmas Eve, she decided to read the Christmas story once again, following the story in the first four gospels of the New Testament. Yet, she could not concentrate, and continued to go to the windows looking out and hoping to see his car approaching through the falling snow – nothing, nothing at all, other than the falling snow. And as the time continued to pass, she became more and more alarmed, wanting to do something, anything, that would help her overcome this worry, this dread, that she felt throughout her entire being. She needed to keep busy, then looking up at the clock and said. "I'm sorry kids, but he's not here yet, and it is time to go to bed." There was some grumbling, and complaining, after all it was Christmas Eve, and that meant that there would be no presents under the tree unless they went to bed.

She herded them off through the nightly routine, of getting into their pajamas, brushing their teeth, and saying their nightly prayers. All she could do was put on a front of confidence, and encourage them, even though with every passing minute the dread increased. *I need to talk with someone.* She thought as she left the bedrooms of the children. *This not knowing . . . it's just killing me.* She headed back out to the living room and the windows that overlooked the driveway. Sitting down in the big easy chair she picked up the phone and called her mother who lived half a day away. She really needed to talk. Listening to the ringing on the phone it reached the fifth attempt and she almost gave up when it was answered.

* * *

After hanging up she felt somewhat better. She had poured out her heart, with the fears that she had held, and had cried for a short period of time. Now sitting in the easy chair all she heard was the ticking of the clock that was over the mantle of the fireplace, the friendly crackling of the fire, and all around her the soft yellow glow of the lights in the room. She had unplugged the Christmas tree, as it seemed to be cheerful, and it was something that she was not. Staring out through the window she found that her eyes were becoming heavy and it was hard to stay awake, but she vowed that she would.

* * *

She saw that she was in her flannel nightgown, one of her favorites – but instead of being in the bedroom and getting ready for bed she found that she was outside, barefoot, and walking in the snow. But even though she could see and feel the cold, she felt warm and unconcerned that she was dressed this way. It did not make sense, but at the moment she had no answers. She found that she was covering a vast distance in a short time, again, an impossibility, but again, she did not feel that this was wrong. She suddenly found herself looking at a point on a familiar road, but not remembering exactly where this was, and could see that a car had left the road at this spot.

Without knowing how she now found herself beside that car, but could not approach it. She recognized it immediately. It was her husband's car, and it was almost destroyed. She choked with anguish when this was revealed to her. Then looking inside she saw him there, broken and dying. Oh how she longed to reach out and comfort him, to touch him, to tell him how much she loved him, but she could not. All she could do is watch. Then she realized that there was someone else in the wreck with him, and realized that it must be a Messenger from God. There could be no other explanation. She thought about what she was seeing and realized that it was very dark, and that there was a soft glow within that car allowing her to see. For some reason God was allowing her to see this, to let her know that she was losing her husband on this night, and that God had sent someone to comfort her man during the last moments he would have on this earth.

She knew that he would not see her, and suspected that she was not here anyway, but through her faith in God and Christ, she was being allowed to see something that one is very rarely allowed to witness. Suddenly it was once again very dark and she knew that the messenger had left. She awoke suddenly and realized that everything she had just witnessed was a dream, but one that had been very real. She knew with a certainty, that her husband and the father to their children would not be home tonight, or any other night, and she wept. What would she, or could she say to their three children? This was supposed to be a time of joy, a time of gift giving, a time to renew the memory of the birth of the Savior, but now what she had just dreamed was too personal, and too painful. How could she go on when her soul mate would be gone?

Reaching for the Bible she began reading the words of comfort that lie within, but found that the words were blurring to become unrecognizable as the tears began to flow once again. The comfort and confidence that she had in herself seemed to be fleeing her as a rabbit runs from the wolf. She, once again wept with a heart rending depth of pain and sorrow. Looking up she saw her oldest daughter standing next to her with real concern, but remaining silent. She reached for her and hugged her desperately, and said in very quiet and small voice. "God revealed to me tonight that your father has died in a car crash, and will never come home to us again." Seeing the shock in the daughter's eyes, all she could do was cling to her, and the daughter gripping the mother in her own desperation, and there they remained this way for an unknown amount of time. And then smiling a sad smile the mother said, "We must do the best we can; after all, your father would have wanted it that way. And I know because of what God showed me tonight, that while I am sure what is ahead of us will not be easy, He will always be there for us. Just like your father would have been, if he could."

A Darkness Incomplete

Author's Notes

Almost one hundred percent of my stories, be they short or full length novels, begin with images in my mind, and this one is no different. For most of the Christmas stories I write I begin to come up with a direction or subject a few months ahead so that I have time to do the necessary editing, or if the story doesn't live up to what I expected, enough time to write a new one.

Here's the imagery for this one: It was night and we are in a residential area in a small city. It is rundown and most of the homes that still have residents show signs of age and lack of upkeep. The windows are boarded and very little light leave these homes. There's a damp misting fog that makes the cold night even colder. What street lights still function only highlight the darkness and depression that permeates the area. Many no longer function, leaving the ones that do providing pools or islands of light that is almost immediately absorbed by the mist and darkness.

The streets are patrolled by both foot and vehicle, and there's a permanent curfew that states no civilian can travel at night. To do so risks arrest and incarceration. Into this scene I see an old man making his way down the broken sidewalks with a specific destination in mind.

And with this image or these images I then wrote, A Darkness Incomplete. Still one must remember that with almost all of my Christmas stories I write expect them to come from a different direction than the standard "feel good" stories that one normally associates with this season.

A Darkness Incomplete

It was a quiet cold evening, with the promise of rain or snow in the breeze, as the old man quietly made his way down the street. The homes along this street were run down, and need of paint and repair a very long time ago. All the windows that faced the street were boarded up so no light escaped. It was late, past the mandatory curfew really, but he remained in the shadows and moved with a stealth that defied his age. *How long has this been in effect*? He wondered. While his memory wasn't nearly as good as it once was he couldn't remember when it hadn't existed. Heck he couldn't even recall the event that had led this government to place martial law over all the citizens. Well, whatever it had been it turned out to be the excuse that the government needed to make it permanent. Slowly, over time, their freedoms had disappeared until it was like they were in prison – too many spies, too many willing to turn in someone else to get the pressure off of them. The secret police were relentless in the pursuit of imagined or real crimes, and there was no protection for the common citizen. They had no rights, no guarantees of a fair trial, or a trial at all. No way to confront their accusers or false witnesses. *Just what happened?*

This had been a place where individual freedoms abounded, but now there were none. It used to be the *Land of the Free* – what a joke now. What the State wanted, the State got, and there was no higher authority to appeal – so one tried to stay out of the eyes of the State. Once the State became aware of you, then, likely or not, you would disappear, never to be heard from again. So why was he chancing this tonight? It made no sense really. He was in his eighties and could walk, but to run would be a joke and be all but impossible. So he quietly shuffled, continued to remain in the shadows, and move cautiously from shadow to shadow. These existing shadows caused by the lack of street lights as only one in three seemed to function, and of those that did, the light produced was dim. Oh yes the ones who were in control had night vision goggles, police dogs, and the many patrols. But after a while the patterns came to one, and if one was very careful, one could move from one place to another and not be seen, not be caught. As he passed a dingy street lamp he glanced at his watch – a gift from the past – and knew that he needed to be inside in the next few minutes as the next patrol was due. So he headed around the dilapidated and abandoned house, avoiding the wet grass and seeds, then through the broken door that led to the basement and entered just far enough to remain out of sight – hidden.

He heard the vehicle and could see the spotlight light up the yard between the houses. It lingered for a moment; he could hear the police vehicle idle for a few moments. He held his breath as he wondered if he had left some evidence of his passing. He slowly let out his breath and continued to breathe with shallow slow breaths. Finally the light moved on and then he heard the car pull away. He knew that he needed to continue his waiting because there would be a foot patrol on the heels of the mounted one. Still, as cold as it was, he suspected that they would move as quickly as possible and head back to the warmth of the station. Tonight the cloud cover was hanging low touching the tops of the lamp posts, producing a light fog that further obscured the light, deepening the darkness, and there was a very light mist falling furthering the shadows even more. Yes, he was cold, but it wasn't the first time, nor would it be the last. He couldn't remember the last time that the room that he lived in was warm. *Again, what happened?* If he remembered right, and who knew if he did, as he found his mind playing tricks on him all the time, after all age could do that to one, it had been rare that his home had been cold. There had been enough firewood, enough electricity, and enough gas to keep one warm. But as the time slipped from the past to now, these things became rare, except, of course, for the ones in charge. One could look, with envy, when passing their homes, or places that they worked. It was quite obvious that they had what all used to have.

Taking a deep breath, now that the foot patrol had passed, and as he had thought, rather quickly because of the freezing weather, he returned to the shadows and continued down the street. Soon he would leave the streets and head through the wooded area and the destination for this night. *Who'd thought that I'd be doing this kind of thing,* he thought, because if he was caught he knew that death wouldn't be far behind because the state looked upon what he was doing as treason. *Never in a thousand years,* he thought. But here he was, and before him lay the darker shadows marking the beginnings of the wooded area. It would be another fifteen minutes before he reached his destination. And if any observed his destination it would make no sense, none at all. Because where he was going there appeared to be nothing – no buildings, no campgrounds, nothing but the heavy dark woods. Yet, these others would be wrong. He knew that soon his time on this earth would be at an end. After all it was the way of things. You were born, you lived your life, and then you died. It was important what you did with that time between birth and death. Yet how many thought so in what they now faced? He really didn't know, and if the truth be told, he really didn't care. *After all, each is responsible for one's own path or way.*

He felt it in his bones that this would be his last year anyway. But none can predict such things, unless, of course, one became the interest of the government, of the State. Then you could almost predict when your death would come. Nobody spoke of it, but all knew. Still he felt that his time of passing would be because of his age and not because of this government and its suppression of all that is right and good. So with these thoughts he disappeared into those woods, away from the patrols, away from this small city, alone, into the fog with the cold, mist, and darkness as his only companions. Yet if there had been light for someone to see they would be surprised, because he had a smile, a look of joy, the belied the facts, the conditions, the suppression that all of them lived under. So he continued his slow shuffling walk with a determination the defied his frail body, finally walking around a small copse of trees and disappeared from sight.

Ahead of him stood a small group that like he had arrived at this very spot one at a time. No one spoke as each acknowledged the other with a simple nod of the head. Then as a group they entered an abandoned, and completely forgotten mine, the entrance completely hidden, and partially collapsed. Down they went and where the tunnels split they took the direction the held no promise of safety or of wealth – only the promise of a dead end. When they turned the final corner the shaft opened up to a larger area, a room of sorts.

Here candles were lit, here there were benches. In front stood a podium – the benches were filled with people – people who were looking expectantly at him as he headed to the front, towards that very podium. He returned their stares and smiled. Quietly he spoke, "Welcome all, for this is a very special night. One that is most important. Even though very few accept it we know the truth. And this government or any government cannot hide from it or cause it to disappear. For you see, we know that tonight, this special night is the night that we celebrate the birth of our Savior, Jesus Christ. It is Christmas night, and a time to share that good news. So we will read of this from the Bible, have our fellowship, and then return to the world that Satan owns. God Bless you all." And as he walked up to that podium his mind drifted back to those times where each house had trees decorated for the season, and the happy children waiting with impatience for those gifts that would magically appear under those trees. Not knowing or understanding that these gifts were a representation of God's Love. His Love for a fallen people and that this night was the celebration of God reaching out to man so that he could find his way home.

Storms

Author's Notes

Storms, what can I say? First off, I can say that I am a veteran and spent twenty five months in Vietnam. So I missed those family holidays as I served my country. I felt it only fitting that I write a Christmas short story dealing with our soldiers. It seems that every generation have their wars, whether they are called that or not, they must face.

And because of the part of the world where these wars are taking place I brought the story forward to reflect what is happening now. Yet, when we truly think about it, this affects more than just the soldier. There are the loved ones who are praying that he or she will return to them unharmed, but war being what war is, too many never return or return to their families only to be placed in a grave.

It was with these thoughts, my personal experiences and wanting to present a more accurate picture that "Storms" came about. No the story is completely fictitious as well as the setting. It was after the short story came out that I received feedback from people who wanted the rest of the story. So this led to "Storms the Rest of the Story". Here I present both short stories for your reading pleasure.

Storms

It was close to the holidays and they were expecting their son home for Christmas, but instead there came an official letter stating that he was missing in action – from the highs of anticipation, to the lows of despair, all in that few moments of time. *What had happened, is he still alive, had he died?* So much went through their minds as they clung together. This was supposed to be his last tour in that war torn country, in that desert. And once back his time in the military would have been over. They had anticipated a joyful reunion instead of this – this letter. It was to be a rare time that the whole family would be together once again. Through a breaking voice that showed she was holding back the tears Jan asked quietly, "So where do we go from here, what can we do, should we let everybody know?"

Her husband Mike could only shake his head. He had no answers, since this was the very last thing he expected. With a voice as choked as hers he could only say, and at the same time voicing his thoughts, "I just don't know, no ideas, no direction." He was silent for a moment as they continued to hold each other both lost deep in their own personal thoughts, personal grief. After what seemed too long he continued, "I think that there are two things that we need to do. First give this time to be fully realized, and second and probably most important, we pray."

* * *

Corporal Scott Carsen remained hidden in the shallow ravine. This was to be his last patrol before returning home and leaving the Army. At first, as they left the compound, it appeared to be no different than any of the myriad patrols that he had been involved with since being assigned to this company in the desert. Yet, right at this moment, as far as he could tell, he was the only one that had survived the ambush – although, he had no idea if that it would remain that way. The surprise had been complete. The enemy simple rose out of the sands like ghosts and in seconds they were down to only a very few men, and suddenly it had grown quiet and he realized that he was it. With fear penetrating every part of his being he prayed that he might be spared, but felt that with what had just transpired that wasn't going to happen. *Where had the ones who had surprised us come from? And how did they know we would be patrolling this area?* As far as he knew these random patrols were to be just that – random. It was to insure that the chances of ambushes would be minimized. *Maybe, just maybe this ambush had been unplanned. Still I'm not going to find any answers right now.*

With his hastily said prayer a hot desert wind began to blow with determination, and shortly this was followed by a sand storm. Whether it was his prayer, or coincidence that brought the sandstorm, he didn't know. But the one thing he did know was that it was the reason he was still alive. Every once in a while he would see a shadow of one of the enemy materialize out of the blowing sands, and catch a word or two that was thrown by the wind, but other than that nothing. All he could assume was that the ones who had attacked figured they had killed everyone in the patrol. He guessed that the enemy was probably looting the bodies' right at this moment. Well, at least as many as they could find anyway. The only positive thing out of this was that his buddies were dead and they wouldn't suffer at their hands. Still, he knew that if he was captured alive that it would be hell for him, and that a slow painful death awaited him.

He was a Christian in a country of unbelievers who took pride in the fact that they had killed a believer and if he was caught alive . . . well he really didn't want to go there. His thoughts were interrupted when another of the enemy materialized out of the blowing sand, and this time it was obvious that he had been seen. In the dim and scattering light he saw puzzlement on this one's face. This was followed by a smile as the enemy realized that there might be another body to loot. He approached eagerly and carelessly not thinking that the one he was approaching might be alive. After all, their attack on these soldiers had been a complete surprise. He reached down to grab the body and drag it out of the sand, only to his surprise to find this one alive. It was the last thoughts that he would ever have, as he became the victim of a surprise attack himself.

Corporal Scott Carsen, breathing hard after the brief struggle, knew that he couldn't stay where he was. It was obvious that if this one had found him, others would shortly and he couldn't count on being lucky again. He only hoped that the one he had just killed wouldn't be discovered until he was well away. Working his way further down the ravine that he was presently in, he really had no idea where it led or whether there was any safety ahead. All he knew that where he was presently was not safe. At times, as he worked his way away from the area of attack, he found that the shallow ravine almost disappeared and at these points the winds and blowing sand was almost unbearable. The heat was stifling, almost overpowering, and the hot sands that were blowing and the sands he was lying on seemed hotter than the air itself. He felt like he was in an oven. The only respite being the rising walls of the ravine which provided a slight break in the winds and blowing sand.

Finally it appeared that the ravine was beginning to head downhill. Visibility still sucked and he desperately needed a drink of water, but dare not until he could find some place to shelter him from the wicked sandstorm and the possibility of the enemy finding him. Crawling and dragging himself along to remain below the rim of the ravine he felt an edge just ahead of him, and pulled himself up to it. From what he could see, which was nothing really; there was a drop off at this point. Again because of the blowing sands he had no idea how far it down it went. One thing he knew for certain was he couldn't backtrack. He had no idea where the enemy was or whether the body of the one that he had killed had been discovered – leading to a possible search for him. So forward it must be, and after gathering some courage he went over the side, and found that he was falling. It seemed to be a long distance and he screamed, which was lost in the winds and blowing sand and was not heard. He struck something hard, and that was the last thing he remembered as consciousness left him.

* * *

When he finally came back to reality, he realized that his ears were ringing and it appeared to be somewhere close to dusk, but at the same time a thin shaft of bright sunlight was striking him in the face. This initial conclusion had to be false. So where was he? As he began to reason once again he found that it was quiet, and that meant that the sandstorm had blown itself out. Again, where was he? He was about to move when he heard movement and froze in position. Straining to hear he thought he could make out a few words that were in the language of the enemy. Could it be they had figured out that he had escaped and now was searching for him? Well, one thing for sure, he wasn't going to stick his head out of wherever he was and ask. Breathing slowly he studied his unintended hiding place and realized that he was under a rock ledge – probably one of the reasons for the drop off that he had fallen over. He also found that the sandstorm had filled the outside of this ledge leaving only a small crack visible from the outside. Nothing at all to give an indication that there was a hole, a place to remain hidden, or that he was here.

He heard the voices grow stronger a couple of times and had seen a foot a time or two, but no one looked or searched in his direction. Eventually, and he never figured out how or why, he either fell asleep or lost consciousness once again – with the next time of being awake presenting him with total silence and full darkness – he continued to remain motionless. There seemed to be a glow somewhere outside and tried to shift around in the cramped area to location the source of that glow. It seemed to flicker somewhat suggesting that it might be a fire – possibly a campfire. With no success at being able to actually see the source of the glow he knew that he couldn't remain here and carefully removed the sand that blocked the entrance.

Once outside he was able see what had happened. When he had fallen and lost consciousness his body had rolled into this low point. Over time the blowing sand had backfilled the open area leaving only a small opening. From the evidence he figured that the winds cleared and then refilled this place with sand over and over again. Looking towards that glow he saw a campfire and from the shadows and movement within the light he determined that it probably was the same force that had ambushed the patrol he had been part of. Seeing them there he knew that he couldn't remain. Eventually they would discover him and what would follow was something he did not want to experience.

With his eyes adjusted to the darkness he moved slowly down the ravine to a point closer to the fire, crawled up and over the edge, and worked his way away from the camp. He knew or hoped that soon another larger patrol from their base would come out to find out what had transpired, but knew it would take time. The attack had come between check-in times so that left a larger area for another patrol to search – thusly stretching the time necessary to locate the missing soldiers. Now away he stood up and could barely see the location and glow from their fire, and by both compass, and stars headed in the general direction of the base, not knowing what may be between him and safety. He knew that he would have to swing wide into unknown areas to avoid another encounter. What wouldn't he give for that map that Sgt. Gibson had been carrying? Who knew what that item could be worth, but at this moment it probably would be worth anything, anything at all that someone asked for – at least to him.

After a time he came to an area that seemed to be pockmarked with sandstone hills among the sand dunes with a rocky sandy soil that crunched under his boots. Eventually coming close to one of these hills he saw what appeared to be a number of caves that he suspected had been created by the blowing winds, and maybe those rare water events. He wasn't sure if what he was thinking would be a good idea, but he really didn't have a clue to when sunrise would arrive and he felt that it would only be safe to travel at night. Yes, a few of the enemy did have night vision goggles, but not many. And he suspected that the ones that had attacked them probably did not. So he carefully studied his options and felt that one of these caves would give him the best chance of survival. At least he had enough water and rations to last a couple of days if not longer if he was careful. And careful was exactly what he wanted and had to be.

Picking a cave that seemed to give less promise for hiding he checked it out and found indeed that it did offer less promise and had to continue his search eventually finding one similar to the one he had fallen into earlier. With the small flashlight he crawled into the opening, sliding on his stomach for a short distance before he was able to stand and explore this cave, finding this one went back some distance and then opened up into a large chamber. He hoped that the small opening would discourage anybody to more than look and then move on. To his surprise he found a small natural tank – simply a place that happened to be a depression in the stone that over time had deepened – that still held water. These natural tanks were never guaranteed to hold water so one couldn't count on them, and because of this were rarely included as a water source on any of the local maps. He thanked God for this find because it meant that he could stay here for a longer period of time, leaving no tracks, no sign of anyone being around, and probably remain safe. At least with the winds that blew in the desert at night, any tracks that he would have left would disappear before morning. Searching and exploring his new *found* home he set up for the long haul, to wait this out, and he hoped that soon, one way or the other, he would survive.

Even though he had been unconscious for however long it had been, he found that the stress and fatigue of the day was beginning to overwhelm him and he would need to sleep. As had been his habit since a child he prayed. Praying specifically for the friends and comrades that he had just lost – their families – and thanking God for his own survival and that soon, this ordeal would come to conclusion. Once his prayer was complete he thought about taking out that small Bible that he always carried but for this one time decided that sleep was more important – as it was he could barely keep his eyes open. Finding a semi comfortable place in the sands that covered the floor of this hidden place he was instantly asleep.

As he slept a vivid dream entered his mind. It was strong enough that when he awoke that the images remained with him. He found that he was in this very cave where he had found refuge, sitting in the dark. He needed to conserve the batteries in that small flashlight so he was using it sparingly. After all he might be required to remain in this hidden place for an extended period of time and as such had to use his finite supplies sparingly. This included, of course, his weapon and ammo for which much had been used up in that brief and bloody firefight. In a sense that had a positive side, if one really wanted to think about it. It meant that the weight that he was carrying was less. Still by being in the dark all of this was a mental exercise since he couldn't see any of his remaining equipment. He suddenly realized that the light in the cave was slowly changing. It came to him when he began to see his legs, leaving him puzzled for a moment. He was sitting cross-legged on the floor, leaning forward and looking down that way. His back was against one of the walls and when he looked up he saw a man standing by the small natural tank lighting the area with a soft glow that allowed this person to be seen. As for the source of that light he wasn't sure, but it appeared to originate with this individual.

Funny how dreams work – he didn't consider it to be out of the ordinary, and that it should be this way. It was then that this one spoke. He didn't even know how to describe the voice other than the timbre was definitely male. With power and conviction this person, who never identified himself said, "Many prayers have gone to the Father on your behalf and He has heard. It has been tasked to me to inform you of this and that what is transpiring here has already been written, the outcome known, and that this has all been foreseen."

All Corporal Carsen could do was stare. He was just about to ask a question, when this one who was there before him smiled, and darkness enclosed the cave once again leaving him quite alone. *What's this all about?* He thought. It was at this point that he snapped wide awake playing that dream back through his mind a number of times, until exhaustion took him once more and he fell once again into a deep sleep.

It was the sound of vehicles that brought him back to reality. Not sure if it was his imagination he worked his way towards the entrance of the cave and once his eyes adjusted to the change in light he looked out and froze. He knew that he couldn't be seen but he didn't want to make some type of movement that might cause someone to look his way. Here, he found that the place he had chosen to hide was an area surrounded by sandstone hills forming a small bowl. And presently inside of this bowl were a number of vehicles and all of them belonged to the enemy. He heard them speaking among themselves and watched a number of them entering some of the caves higher up, both removing supplies, and storing other supplies. It was now obvious that this was a place that they used quite frequently and it made him fear that they would be aware of the cave his was now hiding. Quietly, he withdrew to the deepest portion praying that the cave that he was in would be overlooked. After all, he was alone and heavily outnumbered. *Out of the frying pan and into the fire*, he thought.

* * *

As was tradition, the family gathered on Christmas Eve. Mike and Jan smiled as they welcomed their other two children, their mates, and their grandchildren into their home. All would remain this year to celebrate

Christmas as a family, and later on Christmas Day return to their homes. While this was a joyful time for what this time of the year represented, it was also subdued, since one of their own was missing. And because there had been nothing said or added since that letter, what had happened with their one missing son was still unknown. And if any wanted to admit it, the normal family tradition was simply to enjoy the family Christmas eve, returning to their homes for that special Christmas morning that is so special for the children. But this one time, they, as a family, had decided to spend both the evening and the next day together.

It was important to them to remember the one missing family member and to lift up in prayer his safe return. Scott had always been one that wanted to join the military even though the rest never understood it. And through the time of basic training and AIT he had thrived. It was obvious to them that he really enjoyed it. Yet, now, at this time of the celebration of the birth of Christ and all it represented, there was a deep sadness that couldn't be hidden even though they tried. So with heavy hearts they turned in, smiling at the excited faces on the children, knowing that tonight there would be too little sleep, and that with dawn, these same children would be out of bed, sneaking into the living room to see what had been left under the tree. And even with the sadness that permeated their beings they couldn't help but smile, as the warmth of memories came flooding back to them of their time waiting, when they were young, with great anticipation, for Christmas morning.

* * *

Ah Christmas morning, the chaos, laughter and joy, as those mysteries that magically appeared under the tree were revealed, one by one. It was now late morning and quiet was slowly returning, with the parents and grandparents sitting around the kitchen table drinking coffee, taking a brief respite as they could. If things followed the norm, then shortly, most of the young ones would be napping, giving them the time to clean up the torn and scattered bright wrapping paper. It would be a time, once again, of remembrances, of nostalgia, of stories, from those times past. It would be the time that all could relax before beginning the Christmas meal that all would share, giving thanks to God for his Son who came to be the Savior of the world.

In one of those quiet moments there came a knock on the front door. All of them looked at each other questioningly as nobody was expected since, other than Scott, all of them were here. Maybe it was one of the neighbors? After all, a number did stop by to wish them a Merry Christmas. Plus they were aware of what was happening with the family. They heard the door being opened by one of the older children followed by a scream of delight. Now curious they started to get up when the child came running in with a big smile beckoning them to come out to the front door. And as they came through the doorway from the kitchen to the living room there stood Scott, home, safe, and with tears and joy they joined him, as he joined the family. Many questions were in their minds as well as on their lips, but for now they kept silent. And before them, on this Christmas day, they were all here, all together, a whole family once again. And God had provided, to this family, a gift. It was a gift of love, of family, the reunion of their son and brother, and there could be nothing better than this. *Unless, it was the gift God gave mankind – and that was the ultimate gift – his Son.*

Scott quietly closed the door, and as a family they all returned to the kitchen, to memories, to family, and he quietly thanked God once again for his safe return home.

Storms – The Rest of the Story

Sargent Franklin stood on the hot sands overlooking the shallow ravine. His patrol had just finished recovering the bodies of the ambushed patrol. It had been an overflight by a UAV that had pinpointed the area of the ambush. This had taken a couple of days of both ground and overflights to find. With no reports coming from the missing patrol it was hoped that there had been something that had transpired that had delayed them and not what was ultimately discovered. Breathing deeply and letting it out slowly, he read what had happened. *The missing patrol didn't have a chance.* His thoughts were interrupted by Private Johnson who was trying to get his attention. Looking up he asked, "Yes private?"

"Sarge, from what we can determine we are one body short. It appears that the enemy has stripped the bodies of anything of value, taken all their ID's, followed by some minor mutilation. We haven't been able to put names to any of them, so we have no idea who's missing."

"Okay, I'll get a vehicle out here so we can return

our fallen back home. That sandstorm that blew in will complicate things. I can only hope that he wasn't captured by them. If he had then he's dead now and we can do nothing. So let's hope that either he's here among our dead and we haven't found him yet, or he escaped." Sargent Franklin worked his way into the ravine and helped move the bodies out of the ravine so that it would be easier and more efficient to place the dead into the vehicles. Besides, his soldiers needed something to occupy their time, and to keep their minds off the tragedy that lay before them. He knew that once this was accomplished that they would need to do a more thorough search followed by a sweep outward if they didn't find the missing soldier.

They had been out in the field searching for a few days with no success until the overflight of the UAV had finally located the missing patrol. Even still, until they had actually reached the site of an obvious ambush and it was only then the worst had been confirmed. From the images that were provided by the UAV, nothing could be determined for sure. They didn't know if this location was the location of the missing patrol. It was because the bodies had been partially buried by that brief sandstorm making them almost unidentifiable. Leaving it almost impossible to know whether what they were seeing were bodies of the enemy, or the missing patrol.

* * *

Corporal Carsen remained where he was, not venturing towards the entrance once he identified what he was facing. All he could do was wait it out and hope that the enemy wouldn't look into this cave. At least if they did, in one sense, he sort of had the advantage. If they found him and decided to attack by coming inside he could take them out as they worked their way inside. The disadvantage lie in the fact that in reality, all they had to do was point their weapons inside the cave and spray the whole area down, or toss a grenade inside. Between the ricochets and flying bullets there would be very little chance of him surviving. So his only real hope was that where he was would be ignored and he would remain undiscovered.

He stared at that bright shaft of light that marked the entrance and watched as it was broken now and then as someone walked close to the narrow opening. But, to his relief no one seemed interested in looking for him here. Maybe it was because they used this place so often that they considered it a safe area and didn't suspect that one of their enemy was residing within a few feet. At least with the water that the tank provided and the fact that he was remaining here and could reduce his need for food he probably could outwait them – at least he hoped so.

Time dragged and he knew that the sun had set at least twice since his arrival here. Unfortunately, it didn't appear that the ones outside had any inclination to leave. He felt that it might be the increased pressure put on them because of the ambush and increased patrols. They were probably of like mind – no movement, less chance of being found. Yet, it was obvious to him that this was one of their hidden caches and a stopping off point that was used often. Somehow when he had arrived and found his hiding place this was unknown. And from what little he could hear they seemed somewhat relaxed as he heard some joking and laughter every now and then. All he could figure out, at this point, is that he had somehow he escaped the ambush unscathed and was unknown to the enemy. So his flight from the ambush could have been a little less frantic, since he was stuck right here anyway.

He dared not have any light, so remained in the darkness and while restless from the lack of anything to do, he knew better than to move a lot. It was probably close to a week when, in the grayness of dawn, he heard their vehicles come to life. He heard the voices yelling back and forth, and after a short period of time, the sound of the vehicles pulling away and slowly fading into the distance. Still he waited, not sure what he really wanted to do. It was probably midmorning before he carefully worked his way to the entrance and searched the area with his eyes. There was a great chance that someone might remain here and he didn't want to be overconfident, come out of his hole and find himself in the middle of a camp, still filled with the enemy, expecting it to be just the opposite.

Unfortunately his view wasn't good enough to see the entire bowl. This left him in a quandary, now what? Did he dare stick his head out, or should he give it more time? If they were gone he needed to do the same. If they weren't it would better if he remained hidden. *What to do, what to do?* Finally taking a deep breath he slowly slid partially out of the cave to a point where he could see the whole area and to his relief there was nothing but the sand, sandstone hills, the caves, and silence. Briefly he slid back into the cave, took out his small flashlight and made sure he had all of his gear. He had run out of food the day before and with the distance he still needed to travel that might become an issue. Yet, he needed to be away from here. A place that he thought was safe and would be a refuge instead had turned into a trap. He didn't want to remain any longer than necessary now that he knew what was here and that the enemy could return at any moment.

Sliding out of the cave, he stood up for the first time in a week, under the sunlight and breezes of the desert, and it felt wonderful. He had actually become chilled in that cave and the heat from the sun and warm air soaked in. He knew later that the heat would be an issue but not at this moment. Quickly he went to the caves where he saw the enemy place some of their supplies to see what was there, and found that some of the supplies were packaged food which he took. There were rounds for weapons also, but none that would work for the one he carried so with the few that he had it would have to do. Once partially resupplied he reconnoitered the area outside of the bowl and headed out. He would need to find a place to hold up for the day and once again travel at night. The one thing he knew for sure, that it wouldn't be here. It was a place that had come close to being his undoing and he wasn't going to repeat that mistake again. He had quite a distance still to go and the sooner he got to it, the sooner it would be over, one way or the other.

Two weeks later, out of water and food, exhausted and at the end of his strength, he was picked up by a mounted patrol and returned to the base. Once he recovered from this ordeal he received his orders and was looking forward to returning home to his family, thanking God for his survival.

And it Came to Pass

Author's Notes

First off, I'd like to say that this is one of my personal favorites. And while this short story doesn't have any particular individual in mind, I do have something that happened in my past that let me see, so very briefly, into part of the world this story describes. I was seventeen at the time and working my first minimum wage job.

It was at a local small café that no longer exists. I was a dishwasher, or as it's kiddingly stated, a pearl diver. Into that café, one day, a homeless person came in and sat at the counter and drank coffee – it was all he could afford. It was obvious he was looking for a hand-out, which never came. There was more to it but for this story it is unimportant. After he left I never saw him again, yet those images from that encounter have remained with me all my life.

And speaking of images, the ones I had for this story was of a nighttime scene. There was slushy snow on the streets showing the blacktop in areas where the cars had driven. The sidewalks being wet reflected the lights from the brightly lit storefronts decorated for the holidays. Through my eyes I saw a coffee shop, and from this the story was before me. This eventually led to another series of images that all became part of this and in the end completed story that follows.

Think, "The Match Girl", which I've never read, but saw a short done by the Disney Studios long after I'd written this. It was originally written by Hans Christian Andersen around 1845, which means, of course, it was written well before I wrote this short story and the animated short that the Disney Studios created.

And It Came to Pass

Faron sat at the counter of the coffee shop dressed in a ragged suit that was much too large for him. It had been cast off by someone else and he had found it. The suit replaced the clothes he had been wearing, which were not much more than rags, with too many holes including places that made it almost impossible to hide any part of his body. It had been much too long since his last bath let alone having a roof over his head. It was cold outside and before entering the coffee shop he had been shivering from the winds that were blowing. And he had looked, with envy, on the brightly lit stores and restaurants, the decorations that proclaimed the holidays, and even the lights that lit the front of homes where families lived.

It was always difficult making these decisions as to whether he wanted to dig into his paltry reserves of money. Generally coins that he had found on the ground, or in the streets, or on the sidewalks – lost by someone, or because of the minor value of the coin, who didn't feel the need to bend over and pick the coin up. For him it was like gold. But these coins were few and far between, and it took much too long to get enough of them to be of any use. So when misery or the cold penetrated too deeply he always had to weigh heavily the cost of doing exactly what he was doing now. Before him was a cup of coffee, heavily sugared and creamed, since it was all he could afford, and meals in such a place as this were well beyond anything he could afford, even though it was a simple coffee shop.

In rare incidences someone would buy him a meal,

and he was always thankful for those times. But, for now, times were hard for most, and those times, those gifts had become even rarer, as others who had more than he, didn't have enough to give or help. They had their own problems, their families, and even now on what would have been a day where this coffee shop would have normally been full of patrons, talking their small talk, speaking of their plans for the future, or even of today, and what had to be accomplished, were not here at all. In fact, other than him, there were only a couple more individuals. Looking up at the waitress behind the counter he saw a bored individual, since there really wasn't much going on or much for her to do. At the same time he heard a bit of laughter coming from the kitchen as the cooks idled away their time.

He wondered, for the millionth time, how'd he gotten here, and what did his future really hold? He had no answers, and the passing years hadn't been kind, or would the future years – judging by his past – appear to offer anything that would help him out of his present dismal life. He could only count on now, and hoped that he could stay awhile, here inside where it was warm, continuing to drink the coffee, with a cost that had wiped out his small cache of coins. He knew that tonight would be rough. He'd been kicked out of his last place that at least had kept the winds off of him. And as such was on the move once more. A bad time of year to do this, as fall was just about over, and winter arriving fast, with a chance of snow always on the horizon. In fact it was only the calendar that pointed to the change of seasons. The weather had disagreed and there had been snow on the ground for weeks.

He wondered, once again, how and why he ended up where he was. If there had been a way to head south, then what was transpiring at this very moment – the snows, the cold – wouldn't have been an issue. But, for whatever the reason here he was, and most likely, here he would stay. Looking down he could see that his cup was almost empty and he looked over at the waitress signaling a refill. With no look of friendship she came over, grabbed the coffee carafe and refilled his cup. Once done, returned to her place of vigilance to watch for any entering. But it remained quiet, and when he glanced through the glass front, there were few out and about. It was another sign of the bad times.

Christmas was just around the corner, and if he was very lucky he would be able to get a hot meal at the homeless shelter. He wasn't sure. He had tried to get some room there to get out of the biting cold only to find that it was filled to overflowing with "no room at the inn". He had been too late. So here he sat, not wanting to face what lay ahead of him, but knowing he had no choice.

* * *

He was back on the streets with the icy winds blowing the loose snow into small clouds of white that stung when it struck his bare skin. He shivered. The clothing was too little to keep his body warm, and the lack of anything that could be called food had left him with too little reserves to be warm. He needed to find shelter and it had to be now. Otherwise he would become another nameless victim of the cold unforgiving winter. *Even though it's not yet winter*, he thought bitterly. Once again he looked around with envy at the cheerful lights and decorations, but it brought no joy to his heart. How could it? They spoke of hope, of survival, of warmth, of happiness, and he knew none of these at this time in his life.

Eventually he found a place out of the winds – an old broken building that had once been a business. But fire had destroyed most of it, leaving a skeleton – a shell. And since it had never been rebuilt, or torn down, it was as forgotten as he. In one of the corners, this was close to another building, providing a partial wind block, he set up for the night. Faron shivered, and leaned against a shaky wall, and tried to get comfortable. It would be a long night, one with little sleep. Still, with the partially burned scrap that was here, he had built a small fire in a container, and reveled in the small bit of heat it gave him. Fortunately his location and his fire were hidden so no one could come in to roust him or admonish him about his small fire. It would be the only reason he would survive the night.

He itched from being dirty, and his dirty beard showed heavy streaks of gray, giving away his age – showing that he wasn't a young man. And he laughed a bitter laugh when he thought about his past and the fact that this was the very last place he thought he would ever end up. Yet, here he was, and that past seemed more a dream than reality. For now this reality dominated, and controlled his life, as miserable as it was. All he could do was shake his head and ask, why had it gone so bad, why had things changed for the worst, and why was he here? Again, questions he asked himself all the time, but he could never find the answers. And eventually, even though he had blamed others, he knew deep inside that he was here because of his own actions.

Knowing didn't mean that one could change the results, or go back and move in a different direction. If only there was a way to go back and correct those horrible mistakes, the angry retorts, the direction that all of this led, then, just maybe he wouldn't be here now. But, there really wasn't a way to know, to find out. For all he knew what he lived now was what he was destined to live. As he put his bare hands to his small fire it felt so good. He would have laughed back then at such a thought, such a thing as this small fire being the most important thing in the world. He had personally looked down on those homeless, those bums, those in that shabby underworld that was a different place, a different culture, a different way of life and of survival. He was on his way up, and these many forgotten people meant nothing to him at all.

How many years had he lived this life? How long had he been part of this culture? The very one he had turned his nose up and away from so many years in the past. Well, it didn't matter now, he was part of the homeless, part of their world, and the other life was so far in the past it no longer mattered. He wondered, again for the "nth" time why, and if there was a way out. Again, he had no answers.

He knew that the change of direction had happened when he had been drafted, and had gone to war. Before this he was advancing quickly, with a bright future. He spent a couple of years in that war zone, learning about the fears, stress, and depression that was part of such a life. It was there he had begun to drink, and while he no longer did, the alcohol became a means to an end. He became, as so many others, an alcoholic, which led to a dishonorable discharge, and the loss of any chance of returning to his place of work. Soon after that his wife left with their one and only daughter, and he continued to blame everybody for his personal failures. But now, these so many years later, he truly knew where the blame lay. Was it too late to make a fresh start? Would any trust him? He had no answers, and nothing to offer. So at this moment he stared beyond his small fire into the ink black darkness where the only light that penetrated was the light from his small fire.

At least he had the hot coffee earlier so his stomach wasn't complaining too much. Taking a deep breath he covered up with a couple of threadbare blankets that he had rescued from a dumpster. It had been close to where a family had been moving away to who knew where, and they were throwing away, as far as he was concerned, treasures. Yes most were well worn, but when you had nothing, then you looked at such things differently. He remembered watching, hoping that others were not doing the same thing. And when night fell he rummaged through the dumpster recovering things he could either use or barter with to get something he really needed. *Had that been a year ago?* Yes, it had because it was coming onto winter at the time he picked this stuff up.

Shivering when the cold winds found a way into his shelter he fell into an uneasy sleep and hoped to see the morning.

* * *

He awoke with a start. It seemed strange, and considering the cold, it felt warm and comfortable. *How can that be?* He slowly opened his eyes to find that he was in a big bed, and he was on his side turned towards the wall with a curtained window. At this moment in the twilight between asleep and awake, it felt right. At that moment thoughts came unbidden into his mind telling him that *no, this can't be right.* Wasn't it last night that he lay shivering in an abandoned burned out building? Yet, at this moment he didn't care what his mind told him. He looked at his hands and they were the same ones he had seen the night before. Not young, showing the years of labor, of being outdoors, not a life of offices.

It was at this moment that he heard someone turn over and sigh. He froze for a moment. There was a woman in this bed with him. How long had it been since such had been the case, let alone being in such a bed? He was afraid to turn over and see who it might be. Then he heard as well as felt her shifting in the bed and coming closer to him, snuggling up to him and putting her arms over him. She asked him a question, "So why is it that once a weekend comes around that we can't sleep in?"

Sleep in? What's she talking about? Weekend? He hadn't considered days as any more than days for years. It was then he realized that the body that was up against him was naked, and that was another shock. Again, this was something that hadn't happened, well, since he and his wife had divorced too many years in the past. Yes, there had been brief encounters over the years since that time, but none of them were in such settings.

Again she sighed, kissed the back of his neck, stretched and said, "Why don't you go push the button on the coffee. I need to take a quick shower. Then we can talk a little before the day really begins and the kids show up with all their chaos and demands." She hugged him and wrapped her legs around him in a teasing way slid away from him to her side of the bed and he heard her get out of bed.

With all that had been happening he had been afraid to move, afraid that what he was feeling, what he was experiencing had to be a dream. But it felt too real. He slowly turned over and watched as she retreated from the bed, naked as a jay bird, as the saying went, and disappeared into the bathroom. He felt his body reacting to the situation, and yet he was incredulous to all that was happening. He looked around this room, and while it seemed strange, at the same time not. Letting out a slow breath he slipped out of bed only to realize that he was naked also. So that meant they probably had made love the night before. *Is this her house, her home?*

He found his clothes beside the bed on a chair, got dressed, headed out the door into a hallway that extended in both directions. He automatically turned right, which said to him that he knew this place, and sure enough he found himself at the top of a set of stairs, headed down through a living room into the kitchen, found the coffee pot, and pushed the button. Through the kitchen window he looked out on a different scene than he expected. When he had fallen asleep it was coming onto winter. Yet, looking out of the window spoke of spring. *Why does this house, this home, feel right, feel comfortable? And why, for all things, did I know which way to go and where the kitchen is located? And what happened to winter? Time doesn't shift like this.*

The scene before him was the backyard. It had a grass lawn, with a few trees that moved in the wind. Towards one corner was a swing set, speaking of the children she had mentioned. He noticed and to his surprise, expected a door to be to the left, and it was there. He unlocked it and stepped out on to a deck, a beautiful morning, with the perfume of the flowering plants wafting through the air. It was a little cool, but there was a promise of heat in that coolness. Again, what he was seeing, what he was feeling, seemed right, seemed comfortable, appeared to be familiar. He heard the coffee maker finishing its job and turned to go back in and fill a couple of cups only to hear the woman say, "I've got it. I'll join you in a moment."

He heard the cupboard being opened, followed by the refrigerator, and then the cups being filled. He turned as she came out with her hands full and saw a beautiful young woman smiling at him and offering him one of the coffees. He didn't understand. He had to be at least twice her age. Yet, there was a look of love, of closeness that only is there with strongly committed couples in a healthy, Godly relationship. He stared, not sure, only to see her shy look, looking down briefly and asking, "What?"

He smiled, and shrugged. "Oh it's not you, it's me. Must have had a nightmare last night, and I think I'm still living part of it." He laughed when he saw her reaction, and he put out his arms in denial stating, "No, no not you, but what I'm remembering. And for some reason this seems out of place, out of time, and I feel that I'm still asleep and dreaming. Looking down at his cup he found that it was fixed just the way he liked it, which spoke volumes. So was he dreaming, or what he thought he had been living a dream, and this was the real world? At this moment he had no answers. Suddenly her name came to his mind, she's Kate, and he would tease her, calling her Katie, knowing that she hated that name. How'd he know this?

It was at this point that he noticed that both of them were wearing wedding bands, and they were not new. Now he wondered if this reflected the two of them, or they were actually married to someone else, and were having an affair. Again, this didn't fit. No, they were a couple, they were husband and wife – they were a family. But how was this possible? In that other life – he was calling it that now – it was the time of Christmas, which was only a few days away. He was quite alone, had been for years, was poor to the point of having literally nothing, and had fallen off the grid too many years in the past to even remember when it first happened. So which was real? The one he remembered vividly or this one that had a familiarity, but at the same time seemed out of place, and out of time.

Saying nothing as she came up beside him he found that he put his arm around her, and it seemed natural, felt right. Was this how it was supposed to be? It seemed as the breakup had gotten close that all the two of them – his ex-wife from his previous relationship and he – did was fight. And after all this time, he had to admit that he was probably the cause, and most likely the instigator of those fights. Was this how it is supposed to be, he wondered again. He only remembered the pain, the anger, the fear when she thought he was going to strike her. And then the time came when he returned home to find it empty – he was alone. This was followed by the divorce papers and the final spiral into the worthless life that he had led up until this moment. Again which was a dream and which one was real?

The two of them heard some stirring within the house and Kate sighed, shook her head and said, "I guess our quiet respite is over. Sounds like at least one of the kids is up, which means the rest will follow shortly."

The rest? He only remembered the one daughter. He watched as she pulled away from him and with a reluctance and headed back into the house. He remained trying to understand. It was at this moment a stranger stood in front of him – where he came from or how he got here was an unknown. He felt no fear, and knew that whoever this was, there was no harm here. At first there was only silence – then the stranger spoke. "I'm your guardian angel who has followed you throughout your life. I was told that I could show you this. What you are seeing, what you are feeling, this is what God had planned for you. A loving companion throughout your life with a strong faith in God, raising Godly children, and while not an easy life, one that would help your love and faith grow. Instead the enemy found a way in and destroyed all that was there, all that was to be. Yet, through the years, you still mentored to others, talked of your faith, and unknowingly brought lost souls back to God and Christ."

He smiled once again finally saying after a long silence. "It's time to come home."

* * *

The lights flashed on the police cruiser, and the loud speakers were spouting road conditions, and situations that the dispatcher sent out. The ambulance sat silent with the engine idling, but the lights were not flashing as there was no one to save. The two officers returned to the cruiser with one of them picking up the mic and contacting dispatch stating, "Looks like the weather has taken another one. No, I'd say he's been dead for at least half the night. Stranger, no one has recognized him, and he had no ID of any kind. The ambulance will take the body to the morgue, and, oh yeah, Merry Christmas."

Slowly the scene returned to normal, as the vacant burned out business became empty once again. The ambulance left to deliver the stranger to the morgue, and the police cruiser returned to its patrol. For the one who had come to seek shelter here – shelter no longer needed . . . since he would no longer be bothered by the difficulties of this world – has left, only to return home.

Time Shared Time Lost

Author's Notes

When we are children, and especially young children our understanding of the way of things are quite limited – Limited simply because we haven't lived long enough to gain that life experience that eventually takes that magic out of our lives. Our parents have always been there, and while it seems like they know all and will always be there we learn that this isn't necessarily so or true.

If you've been reading other of my Christmas short stories you know that I approach most from an alternate direction, presenting other than those happy family gatherings. Why, you may ask. Simply stated not everybody has a wonderful and joyful season. And I feel that there are lots and lots of those kinds of stories out there.

The season is most magical for children, and we parents in a sense relive our time as children through the eyes of our children. And once they have grown and are on their own it seems that the magic of the season has left with them. Still it is the way of life as we all go through our personal seasons.

In "Time Shared, Time Lost", I decided that I would write this from the perspective of a five year old child. Now I have to admit that my time as a five year old is at least sixty plus years in the past. So if she appears a little mature, (I really don't think she does) for her age then blame the years that have passed me by.

Time Shared, Time Lost

A few months ago she had turned five. Five! Who'd have thought she'd be so big? Not her for sure. And while it had been a great birthday party with many of her friends, in the end, the day went too fast and he didn't show up. Carie looked up at the big calendar. While she had learned to count it was still hard to do. Still with mama's help she knew that Christmas was only a few days away. And she could feel the excitement building inside. She really hoped she had been good enough to get those wonderful presents from Santa Claus. Yet, if she wanted to be honest with herself, things hadn't been going well. And she knew that while she had tried to be good all the time, well, sometimes things just seemed to go wrong.

She had been four when all had changed. She remembered daddy all full of energy and getting ready to leave on one of his trips. She always missed him when he took these trips. Still with what they had they could talk over the computer (such a big word) and she watched and talked with him like he was on TV, which helped keep the loneliness away. Of course the TV wouldn't talk when asked a question. She could tell that mama didn't like to see him go either, but it had been explained to her that this was part of his job. It was a job that took him away from her much too much. In a sense she hated that job. After all he needed to be here for her, and especially mama. She saw how much mama needed daddy even though much of what they talked about she didn't understand. All they would say to her was "Someday you'll understand". Well, she'd really like to understand now. No not those grownup things she'd overhear now and then, but "why"? Why wasn't he here? Why things had changed and they were no longer living in that nice house with the really big yard. And why had most of the nice things gone away? And mostly why was mama sad most of the time?

She had to admit that she was too. She had tried to help, but being so young she didn't know what to do. So at times she'd crawl into mama's lap and hold on tight. Many times she'd fall asleep because it was so comforting and nice there. And she had to admit she felt safe there too. Maybe mama felt safe too when they were together this way. Looking out the window she could see the snow beginning to fall. The house, part of a duplex she had been told – whatever that was, was cold. Not freezing, but one had to wear jackets in the house. Jackets in the house, she always thought they were for when she went outside. She had complained, but mama had explained they didn't have the money to be able to keep it as warm as they would like. So blankets and heavy clothing became the rule. It made it difficult when one had to really go – so many layers that had to be removed. Still one learned not to wait too long, reducing those embarrassing accidents.

She sighed wishing for some hot chocolate with marshmallows, but it was something she rarely had now – again, that money thing. "Would you like to go out and play in the snow?"

Carie hadn't realized that mama was standing behind her watching her look out the window. Yes it would be fun, but they had moved here only a short time ago and her friends were far away and she hadn't made any new ones yet. She shook her head, while smiling. "No . . . no, I'm fine."

"If you change your mind let me know, okay?"

She had to admit it was tempting. It was always fun to go out and make snow angels, to catch snowflakes on one's tongue, to try to build snowmen, but there had always been a warm house to go back to once one became cold. She was cold enough here inside. So she continued to look out and imagine how it would be. She heard her mother withdraw, and soon heard her doing something in the kitchen. The kitchen was something else that had gotten smaller as well as her bedroom and every room in this house. And there were times they heard their neighbors through the walls. When she first heard them she was surprised, but now she was used to it. Part of the changes since daddy hadn't come home, hadn't come back to them.

She remembered the day when a stranger showed up at the door and could sense the dread from mama. Mama opened the door, and after a brief conversation with the stranger slowly closed the door, stood there with her head against it, and began to cry. She didn't understand. What had the stranger done to do this to mama? She had gone up to her and grabbed her leg trying to get her attention, but it hadn't worked. It was later she learned that the plane daddy had been flying had disappeared, and no one had been able to find it so far. If something wasn't found soon, the searches would be called off. And nobody knew if he had survived the crash or not. So daddy was considered lost. She wondered how a grownup could be lost. It made no sense to her. Maybe it was like when they would be driving around and mama would tell daddy to ask for directions and daddy would say while smiling, "I'm okay, we're not lost".

That first Christmas after daddy "becoming lost" had been really really sad and hard for both of them. But another was approaching and while she hoped for some really nice things what she wanted was for mama not to be sad, and for daddy to come home to the two of them. She knew that both of them had prayed for that to happen last Christmas. Yet here they were alone with each other. Not that she wasn't close to mama, it was, just that they seemed, well, not whole, not complete (another of those big words that she thought she understood). Like part of them was missing or broken and couldn't be fixed. She needed daddy, and she knew in her heart that mama did even more. So once again every night with her prayers she asked God to bring daddy home to them so they could be fixed, and be happy once again. Yet, for all of her prayers there had only been silence.

She wondered if it was her fault. Maybe she wasn't asking right. Or maybe she had unknowingly done something wrong. She didn't know, and she didn't have any answers. So she continued to pray at night before climbing into bed hoping God, as busy as he must be, would hear her desperate prayers and answer them. It would be so nice, so wonderful to see him come back through their front door once again. She then worried, because they were no longer where they used to live that if daddy did come back he'd not know where they were. So she added that to her prayers that when God answered her prayers that God would lead daddy back to them.

The days moved past faster than she expected and suddenly it was Christmas Eve. She and mama went to visit her grandparents, and while there she saw many of her aunts and uncles, with her cousins. She had to admit she didn't know anything about family relationships, or how she was a part of this boisterous (Even though she wasn't sure if she really knew what that word meant.) group of people. Still the house was warm, the food great, and the games she and her cousins played made the time go fast. And yes before they left everyone had a gift to open. Most of the time, she had to admit, she was disappointed with what she got from her grandparents. It was always clothes or something similar. What she really wanted was a toy or something she could play with. At least she had fun with others around her age. Yeah there were older cousins, and she had to admit that many times they'd be mean. Eventually it was time to go home. And even though she didn't want to say or think it she was tired.

Somewhere during the drive home, as she stared out the windshield, (She couldn't see over the front of the car so she was always looking up into the sky.) watching the falling snow, hearing the steady sound of the motor, and the warmth of the car, she fell asleep. She really hadn't wanted to but it wasn't the first time, and she doubted it would be the last. In the distance she felt the car stop, and the motor stopped, leaving only silence. Still half asleep she felt the cold air when mama opened the door and immediately closed it. She heard mama as she crunched through the snow, and felt herself being lifted by loving arms. Drowsily she smiled at the loving face looking down at her and put her arms around her. The next thing she remembered was mama undressing her and putting her in her night clothes. She was asked if she needed to go to the bathroom. She shook her head, and felt herself being put into her bed. She was barely awake. Still she remembered the covers being drawn over her and once again smiled. Christmas was tomorrow, and that was all she remembered as she fell into a deep sleep. Yes she did remember mama saying, "Sweet dreams", before leaving her room, and that was it.

Sometimes, close to morning, she'd have to get up and go to the bathroom. This was one of those times. Maybe she should have gone before bed. But she had been so comfortable, so tired, it just seemed like too much effort. So now she paid for it. More asleep than awake she took care of business and headed back to her room, and her warm bed. On the way she thought she heard voices from mama's room, but knew that now and then mama watched TV, and figured it must be what she was hearing. Back in her room she glanced outside and it was still dark. She shrugged, climbed back into the warm bed, and was asleep almost instantly – whatever she heard forgotten. Morning, and Christmas wasn't too far off, but for now sleep was more important. She burrowed deeper under those covers feeling the warmth and comfort. She smiled in her dreams and anticipation of what waited for her under the tree, even though it was a small one.

Suddenly she was awake and excitement filled her. She glanced out the window and saw the gray of dawn and knew it was Christmas morning. She threw off the covers and immediately regretted it as she shivered from the cold. At least the pajamas had footsies so her feet wouldn't get cold. She grabbed her jacket, and quietly, since she figured mama had to be still asleep – *What's with that really* – snuck out to the living room where the tree was. "After all", she asked herself, "It's Christmas and who can sleep on such an important morning?" She knew she could go look, and she would, of course, pick up the brightly wrapped gifts and see if she could guess what was inside, but knew she would have to wait until mama came out to join her. That waiting seemed like a lifetime as those gifts begged to be opened, begged to become hers.

She heard the coffee maker start and smelled the wonderful smell of fresh coffee being brewed. She had begged, at one time, to taste coffee, and like the vanilla flavoring which smelled wonderful, she learned that it didn't taste anything like it smelled. This was something she'd never understand. How can it be that way? Didn't the way something smells mean that's how it should taste? Anyway, that meant that shortly mama should be getting up and they could open these wonderful gifts together. She glanced out the front window as it became light enough to see outside, and saw that another layer of fresh snow had been added and there were no tracks in it making the world look new.

She turned in anticipation when she heard movement coming from mama's room and went over to sit on the couch eager to get on to the next part of this wonderful morning. And to her unbelieving eyes, and such a wonderful gift and surprise, daddy walked out the bedroom with a huge smile. "Hello munchkin". He held out his arms to her which she gladly ran to as she screamed, "Daddy", hugging him so tight and almost afraid to let go, *God does answer prayers*, she thought as she watched mama come out next. Now they were a family once again. Now they were fixed. And as she put her head on daddy's shoulder as he carried her to the couch, she thought, *It really is the bestest Christmas ever.*

The Ornament

Author's Notes

Since the first year I began my blog, I've written a Christmas short story. Yet when it came time to write this one I really hadn't come up with an idea or subject for the story. I asked my wife if she had something that might work and she suggested that I write from the perspective of the decorations we place on the tree every year.

If we think about it we talk to our inanimate objects all the time. And there are plenty of cartoons from the early days that animate these items, including, more recently, Disney's Toy Story movies. I guess in some way it would be scary to think that these objects can see, feel, and think, considering what we do to them when we are frustrated. Let alone the language we have a tendency to spout when we can't get that darn thing to function correctly.

As I thought about it, I felt that the best place to begin would be at the establishment where the ornament was for sale. How would such a place appear to the ornament, and how many times would it be handled before it went home with someone? And because there would be others like him inside those retail packages how would this one see the others?

With these questions and the images beginning to

form in my mind I had enough to begin the process of creating this story. And while this one isn't my very favorite, it is close and I really like it. Yeah, I know I'm the one who wrote it so that's no surprise. Well, all I can say is read it and see what you think?

The Ornament

She came running up to the display where I sat. And I could see the sparkle in her eyes, and a soul full of merriment and excitement for the time of year. *She can't be more than five*, I thought, *and probably a bit younger.* In the distance I saw the one who had to be her father coming to collect her. It became obvious to me that somehow in the hustle and bustle that she had escaped his watchful eye. In the distance I saw the one who must have been her mother as she stayed with the shopping cart. In that cart sat an infant, plus one more that had to between this one standing before me and that baby in age.

If I could smile, I probably would have. But, I was of glass, made to look like a shining silver star with a slight gold tint. Like the one that could have been similar to the one announcing the arrival of another child over two thousand years ago. With the bright lights I shown brightly, reflecting that light from the many facets that is a part of me . . . Just the thing to catch a child's eyes, but much too delicate for them to handle. I heard him, the one who had to be her father, say, "Come on honey, mama's waiting for the two of us and we still have much to do. Plus, you know, if we have time, we need to go over and see your grandmother today."

She answered excitedly, "But daddy . . . look! Isn't it pretty?"

He took a quick look that said to me that he really hadn't, and nodded to her. "Yes, yes it is. Now please come back. There are a lot of strangers in the store, and it would be easy for you to get lost." With that he grabbed her hand and pulled her gently in the direction where the rest of the family awaited.

I watched as she resisted, reluctant to leave, but it was also obvious that she really wouldn't disobey and with her head down, said quietly, "Yes daddy." She quickly looked up at him and back at the display where I was and she said with hope, "Can we get one of the stars? Please?"

I could tell from his reaction that this wasn't the first thing she had asked for in the shopping center, and it was also obvious that with the crowds that his nerves were on edge. He simply said, "Look, as I said, we have a lot more to do here today. And if we still have time, and you're not tired, we can come back, okay?"

She stopped for a moment, and then looked back to me with a big smile and said, "We will be back, and then I can take you home with me and put you on our Christmas tree."

I thought that it would be something which wouldn't happen. With so many bright and shiny things to draw the attention of one so young, she would forget and it would simply be a brief memory for me . . . but I was wrong. Don't get me wrong, with as many who had looked and with the crowds there was a great possibility that some other person or child would pick me and I'd become part of their personal family and history. Yet, as the day moved on, and many of my brothers were chosen, I remained. Why, who knows, I surely didn't. Still it must have been providence, or whatever word you like, for me to remain.

With the time of year all the stores remained open

late, but even so eventually they would close down for the day. After all, the ones who worked here had families of their own, and they deserved to return to them at the day's end. It was close to closing, and the crowds in the stores had thinned when suddenly in the distance I saw them. To be surprised was an understatement. I could see the weariness in the parents. I mean think about it. Running all day through the many stores with young children who would become overly tired and cranky as it is called, besides all the crowds. Well, I'd give it to them. I really felt they'd have gone home a long time ago, probably stopping off and picking up something to eat so nothing had to be prepared once they got home. And I honestly suspect the children – all three of them – would be fast asleep from that ride home.

With a big smile on her face she pulled a reluctant father back over to the display where I remained. I could see by his reaction that he was surprised that I was still here, and I suspect that he had promised his daughter that if I was still available that yes, they would buy it for her. So with care he lifted her up and she carefully picked me up and gently carried me back to their shopping cart where I became part of the many items. I guess I was to be a part of this family and only this family and thusly why I hadn't been picked earlier in this day. As we wheeled out into the parking lot I felt the fresh cold air as all the numerous bags of treasure were placed into the trunk of their car. But, she wanted to hold me and so her father carefully dug me out and had her sit in the car, followed by being safely strapped in before he handed me to her.

I looked up and saw the excitement in her eyes, but she yawned so I suspected she'd be asleep soon. Still before we really got on the road to where they lived they pulled into a drive-thru and ordered their dinner. She carefully placed me on the seat between her and the baby. She quietly admonished the baby to "not touch", and happily grabbed the burger, fries, and drink, and began to eat them telling me all about her day. And as we headed down the road I saw that she was trying hard to stay awake. But the food, the excitement of the day, plus the quiet droning of the car was winning and as hard as she tried, she lost the battle and soon was sound asleep as were her siblings. I saw the mother look back and smile a loving smile and say something to her husband, where he whispered something back. And by the lateness of the hour I felt they would be heading home instead of going over "to grandmother".

I really couldn't see out from where I sat but I did see that the side windows were frosted telling me it wasn't warm and soon I heard a change as we pulled off the interstate and onto the side roads. I heard the windshield wipers rhythmically slapping the car as they cycled trying to keep the windshield clean and clear. Eventually the car slowed more and then pulled into a driveway where it stopped. They left the car running with the heater on and one of the parents left and I guess unlocked their door to the home where they lived. Then one by one they took the children inside. Yet before they could take the little girl she awakened slightly reached down and picked me up hugging me to her breast and then her father carried her inside with the mother shutting down, locking up the car and following behind.

They took her to her room, got her into her night clothes – you know those pajamas with the footsies – had her take care of the bathroom routine and tucked her in her bed. Looking up she reached out hand hugged her father saying, "I love you daddy." For which he smiled a tired smile saying, "And I love you too sweetheart." At this point he handed me to her since it was obvious she wasn't going to let me go. At this point she snuggled down deeper under her covers, sighed a contented sigh, and was almost instantly asleep. I watched from where I was as he smiled a loving smile, making sure she was tucked in, and quietly left the room, turning out the light and closing the door. Still there was a nightlight so the room wasn't dark. I knew they – the parents – still had to unload the car, plus all the other responsibilities they had to do before they would retire. I thought about this sleeping child where I remained. *Yes to be young and innocent, to not understand what the world really is, to think what little I see and understand to be the world, and feel safe, such a wonderful thing.*

I knew as he put his daughter down for the night that she, her mother would be doing the same thing for the middle child and I suspect that together they'd get the baby to bed before heading out and finishing the night. Yet, for me it simply is a guess since here I am in this bedroom with the one who'd chosen me.

* * *

It was the next day and for a while I remained in her bedroom. It seemed she had much to do and at this time it didn't involve me. I guess it is the standard stuff, but you must remember I hadn't been around such before. I learned she had to go to the bathroom, take a quick bath after getting out of her pajamas, and from the laughter and splashing I could tell she, and later I learned her younger brother had a good time playing in the water. From where I was I heard screams of laughter as the sounds got closer to her bedroom and she ran into her room with her mom close on her heals. She jumped on the bed naked as a jay bird, as the saying goes, throwing the towel she had with her on the floor. I saw her mother shaking her head, even though she had a smile on her face. "Okay, little one, it's time for you to get dressed and then we need to go downstairs and have breakfast." It was quiet for a moment as the mother appeared to be listening and whatever she heard caused her to shake her head.

At this point she turned around and went to the door and yelled down the hallway. "I have this one, you take care of your son, and then we can all head downstairs and get some food." Whatever the answer brought laughter to her lips. She turned around and her daughter was still on the bed daring her to make her get dressed, but in a fun way as there was a sparkle and challenge in those eyes. I could see that this was a familiar game the two played and with much tickling of the daughter and laughter from both of them the mother finally got the girl dressed, had her sit on the bed as she brushed her damp hair, and again it was obvious this young one didn't really like having her hair brushed.

Soon they disappeared downstairs and for the longest time I knew nothing and heard nothing. Then she ran back into her room came over to where I was and carefully picked me up and said, "It's time. I get to put you on our Christmas tree!" When we left her room I could hear, in the distance, what sounded like music – Christmas songs and such. And as we reached the stairs where I could look down I found a room transformed from what I remembered from the previous night. There was garland interwoven in the railing of the stairs, and a big green tree in the middle of what they call the living room. And it was obvious that much time and care had been given to decorating this Christmas tree with lights, bobbles, globes and so much more. But at this moment there wasn't anything placed on the top, the place of honor.

It was at that moment I realized that this was to be my place. To be the one on top of the tree and to look down on all that existed here. If I were a living thing I probably would have glowed and been filled with pride for such an honored place. I watched as she handed me to her father who then unpacked me carefully from the packing that protected me from being broken. I saw the impatience on her face as he took his time. Looking up I could almost see a hidden smile saying to me that he was deliberately being slow, and watching her and her impatience. Finally when he could tell that she had almost reached her end he handed me over. She reverently took me in her two small hands and her father lifted her up and with care she placed me in this place of honor. She studied me for a few moments, made a slight adjustment and then told her daddy she was done. He carefully set her down and tickled her a little bit getting the expected giggle.

He looked down and asked. "So what do you think?"

"Oh I think the star is won-der-ful, and just right!"

I could tell that the big word was something she said with some difficulty, but I could also see that she was proud that she could say it. I watched from my high perch and he looked up and appeared to be studying me and where I was, paused, looked down, and it was obvious to me that she was waiting for his approval. At this point he crouched down so he could be eye to eye with her. He simply said, "Yes, I agree." At this point they turned on the lights and the Christmas tree shown in its own splendor.

* * *

The days flew by and I saw, as the days passed, the children, at the least the two older ones, were becoming more and more excited. As to the whys I really didn't understand then. Still there was a routine to what happened in the house, and I fell into this feeling comfortable with the love I felt here. Then one night they left – all of them – and this was different. Yet it had become obvious that something important was about to happen. I heard something about going over to the children's grandparents as it was a tradition they did every Christmas Eve.

Now I knew that I had been created for this time of the season, but really didn't understand the significance of what it represented. In fact it took a few seasons for me to put it all together, and then it all made sense. It represented a time of giving. And while it appeared to be a magical time for the children, it really was much more serious than it appeared. It was a couple of conversations the parents had that finally put it all in perspective. This time of the year represented the ultimate gift – God bringing man back to Him through the gift of His Son. This led to the understanding of the gifts magically appearing under that tree. That same tree where I sat on top, but I get ahead of myself since this is the first year or season I became a part of their tradition.

The house was quiet and seemed empty while all of them were gone. And while the lights that lit the tree were normally on at this time, they weren't at this moment, and a soft glow from the hallway light was all that could be seen. It was hours later when I heard the car park in the driveway and the key open the lock. This was followed by the daughter being carried in by her father sort of half asleep. She looked over at the tree and me, and I could make out a huge smile and it was obvious she was anticipating something. Again what this was all about I hadn't a clue. Her father carried her up the stairs and I suspected to her room, then returned and with a practiced routine returned with the son and the mother carrying the baby.

The next hour or so seemed to be involved in getting the three to bed and tucked in for the night. Then they came downstairs and went into the kitchen where they turned on the light, made some coffee, and sat quietly and talked. It seemed, to me, that all was right with the world at this moment. I heard the chairs scrape the floor as they were pushed back and I watched the parents head upstairs. I thought they would go to bed also, but I was oh so wrong. I heard them whisper something and then, as if by magic many wonderfully wrapped gifts appeared under the tree. I noticed, for the first time that a plate had been left out and there appeared to be some cookies on it with some kind of note propped up. And like the gifts appearing, the cookies magically disappeared, and a new note replaced the one that had been left. Then it was quiet, quiet until just before dawn.

I thought I heard a creaking of the floor, and I saw her quietly come down the stairs wide-eyed and full of wonder. She carefully looked at all that was there – all the brightly wrapped gifts and presents. She tentatively picked up a couple. If it had been lighter in that room I probably would have seen that huge smile, and probably a lot of impatience. I suspected that she had to wait until everybody was up, and right at this moment she knew she was the only one. So she went over and sat in one of the big chairs and tried to wait. Again, it was obvious she was too excited to be able to sit still. So she headed into the kitchen, and kind of walked around trying to make that old clock go faster, but nothing seemed to work.

I could see that she thought, a couple of times, that she heard someone moving upstairs, but each time it turned out to be nothing. Eventually, and it was still before dawn, she saw her brother at the top of the stairs rubbing his eyes and looking like he had just awakened. She looked up at him and whispered he needed to be quiet, and come down and see what Santa had left them. So, with care taking one step at a time he came down, and I saw that incredulous look that he couldn't believe what he was seeing. Now taking on the role of her mom she told him he could look but that's all, until momma and daddy came down to join them. Now I had two impatient kids waiting and it was obvious it seemed to be killing them.

Eventually I heard the coffee machine begin its daily ritual of making coffee. This only heightened the anticipation for the children as they knew their parents would put in an appearance shortly and then they could find out what awaited them behind all the beautiful wrapping paper. Yet, I learned this day they had a family tradition where fresh cinnamon rolls would be baked, and with coffee for the parents and milk for the children they would gobble the food down before the father would become the official gift giver as he would look to each package, read the name on it and hand it to the new owner. And they had to wait until all of those wonderful gifts were piled in front of them. Then they'd each open one and show all what they got, and continue until all of them were open.

I saw, from the squeals of excitement, and the joy that these items they received were loved things, and soon with Christmas music playing in the background, each child began playing with their new treasures, and quietly, since there had been gifts exchanged between the parents, it was time to clean up all the torn and beautiful wrapping paper, plus all the boxes these gifts came in. And as the morning progressed I began to see yawns on the young ones, and with urging from mom and dad, they took their gifts to their bedrooms and soon it was quiet. I saw the mother and father look at each other and smile. For a while it would be quiet and they could relax before working to put together that final Christmas meal that they all would share later that evening.

And then, it was over. As a new year dawned everything got packed away including me. So until it became that time of year once again, I would know nothing of what happened with the family. Again that is the way it should be since I am to shine during that special time of year. Still this isn't the end of the story. I guess we could say so but that leaves so much out, and so much that is important. Still I have to admit that very first Christmas that I participated and remembered will always be special to me. But I digress and it's time to continue . . .

Now I feel that it's important that I cover that first Christmas season in much detail, but to continue to do so really would make no sense. Yet I remained an important part of the family for years to come. I watched the change in the little girl as she grew. And each year she became less and less of a child, until she became what her parents called a pre-teen. I began to notice a change and while she still placed me in the position of honor on the top of the tree, it seemed to be more of a chore instead of a privilege. Still all things change, and believe it or not even me. I now had a few scratches, nicks, and such even with the careful handling. Still I felt the love in this house and the care they gave to everyone and everything.

Then one year a few after this one she was gone, and only her brothers were home. I found that the mother and father now placed me on top of the tree, and the two boys helped with the rest of the tree. Yet, once again, I felt the changes that were in the air. I didn't know what to attribute these changes to, but realized it had to be because the young ones were no longer young. And then all the children were gone and it was only the two. And while I felt the love, it seemed the magic was gone.

It was during this time that the children would show up for an evening – not all, all of the time – before returning to wherever they lived. I realized that the ones who lived here, well, their hair had turned gray, and they seemed to move a bit slower. It surprised me that so much time had passed. Then in the middle of one of those years, where I normally remained packed safely away, new changes happened. Suddenly I, with everything in this house, was packed away and this house with so many happy memories became empty. The mom and dad moved away from this home and into something much smaller. I guess it made sense because they really had no need of all that space.

It felt strange that first Christmas in this new place. I knew nothing about or of it. It was then I realized that when the children came to visit, that they had children of their own, and of course soul mates – all beginning a new tradition for each new family. And it was then I found that I was removed from the tree top and given to the daughter, the one who originally spied and wanted me so long in the past. So I left this home and went to a new place. I saw as I was carefully packed into the car that she rode while her husband drove. I heard the sounds of a baby, and knew I would be seeing another family grow.

* * *

And yes I did. I watched as the magic returned and her four children grew, and like when she left I saw her family leave. And on a sad note I also knew that her parents had passed making her the matriarch of her family, as well as her younger brother who became the patriarch. And, for whatever the reason, it seemed that none of her children were interested in me – those two girls, and two boys. Yet, as I had seen it happen to her parents, I saw the gray beginning, and suddenly she was alone as she lost her soul mate. It had been just before Christmas, and while I ended up on her small tree, I knew it was a sad time for her.

* * *

And yes, life goes on, and I got to see it renewed as her children found loved ones and had children of their own. It meant that most likely that I would see an end to my beginning, to see the one who had chosen me so long ago join her parents, and her husband, but that is life. Yet, before I witnessed any of this, one of her granddaughters fell in love with me, and I could see, while the one who had chosen me so long ago was reluctant, she passed me on to her granddaughter. Where I became special and once again held the place of honor . . .

Yes, I wondered what happened to my brothers who had become part of other families, but this is something I will never know. Still, I consider myself blessed with all I've seen in those snapshots each and every Christmas. I learned of love, and what it meant, and what it does. I learned the importance of family and the ties that keep them together. So as an ornament what more can I ask, other than to continue being a part of something so great. And I guess this is my story. So God Bless to you and yours, and Merry Christmas!

The Child

Author's Notes

I write mostly in the Science Fiction/ Post-Apocalyptic genres and as far as a Christmas short story I hadn't. So in 2017 I decided to remedy that and wrote, "The Child". If we think about it whenever we, as a species, change our location, be it during the times of the great migrations on this planet, to the fictional expansion to other solar systems and habitable planets we always carry our traditions and roots with us.

It is such that allows us to remain connected to not only our past, but to our ancestors, and each other. While we have an overall connection to our culture, within this we have those special traditions that can only exist within families. It is what makes us, well, us. The myths and legends, and history, be it personal or worldwide define us. So where this story takes place might be anywhere in the universe.

As always this led to the images in my mind that became this story. And if you haven't figured it out, if you were to look back on my short stories they are mostly written in the first person. This one is no different. The only difference is here we have a brother talking about the past, his younger sister, a little about where they live, and his family. If you have siblings then you know of what I speak. There is much in those relationships that will always be with us.

The Child

She is my sister, the youngest of the family. She's known as En to us, but to the community, the place where we live, she's known as *the child*. I guess a little background here would let you know what this is all about. First off the one telling this story is obviously me. And my name is Fe. I've been told that it means iron, and because of the fact that only half of my siblings survived I was given that name in hope that it meant I would survive. I'm one of three surviving children of my parents and being the oldest put more responsibility on me. But to be honest it wasn't a position by birth, as I was the second born.

My oldest brother only lived days before succumbing to what I've never known. I just know that whatever it was, in the end it took two others. Had we all lived then I would have been part of a family of eight – my sires or parents, me, three brothers and two sisters. Instead there was just my younger brother, and then the youngest being En. And because of the tragedy of family we've always been close.

I remember the day my sister came into the world and we, my brother and I heard the cry of a newborn coming from the room where mom had just birthed her. And shortly we were invited in to meet her. It was there for the first time that we learned some of the differences between females and males. Of course there's much more to this, but at our age such was of no importance. Both my brother, and me thought that there had to be something wrong with this baby as she lay naked on mom's chest. She was missing something between her legs and it was such a surprise. I mean I remember when my brother came into the world and he had what I had. So I or we thought that this was how every baby was.

Mom called both of us over – dad was there next to her and smiling – and we were shy about it. With the tragedies that had happened we really didn't want to mention this obvious defect. But I guess moms can read their children because it seemed like she knew what we were thinking and smiled as she said, "Meet your new sister. We have named her En." There was a pause and I could see she was trying hard not to laugh. Then she said, "This is the way girls are. It is one of the differences between you and her." Mom did laugh lightly, although we saw that it hurt. "Later . . . much later you will see other changes that make girls different, but for now this will be the only one."

Well, I had to admit, at that moment, it was a big difference. But after a short time it was something we didn't even notice. Only that as she got older, began to walk, and get into our personal stuff, we had the normal arguments, small fights, and complaints that all children have. Still, there was something different about her. She was always smaller, well no surprise here since she is the youngest. But even here it seemed as if she would remain small. Then there were her eyes – always large, deep, and bottomless, as if she might see forever. She had a beautiful face that at times looked like mom, and other times reflected some of dad.

It was as she approached her fourth year that the reason for this other difference arrived. She had been given *the gift*. Yet for many who had received this in the past it had been anything but a gift. In fact it was more of a curse. It was when this *gift* manifested itself and was learned by the rest that she became to be known to our small village as *the child*.

Oh, I believe that it's important that I break here and tell you a bit about our village – if one can call it such. Small is just about all one can say. And we are surrounded by desert. From what we've heard this world is almost completely desert. But for me personally I have no way of knowing or confirming this as I've lived here in this village, with the isolation, for my entire life. If we didn't have visitors now and then, coming from other areas that are protected from this great desert, then it would be easy to assume that we were the only survivors.

Don't ask me why I use that word – survivor, because I don't know. I can only say is that the word seems to fit. Maybe a remnant of a greater time in the past, honestly I don't know. All I know is that this line of reasoning seemed right. Did I have any facts to back this up, or was there anything written in our history to support such a thought, no. It was just a feeling that I had. And I guarantee that there will be no way for me to travel beyond our lands. I do not have the time, the resources, or the need to leave and explore the vast desert.

Where we live is in a series of canyons – not large, but for whatever the reason they prevent the desert from encroaching here. To reach our lands, and the precious waters, required one to enter through a narrow passage that led downward into a series of narrow trails which were always shadowed because of the walls that rose to the sky. I suspect it was because of these features that kept the desert out.

Winds always howled down those narrow passageways. And sand would often pile near the entrances to the trails, but for whatever the reason would become less and less as one hiked through. Eventually they would open into the canyons where we lived. There was a small lake fed by a small stream that came from the living rock. And for as long as we had been here it had never failed. We prayed that it would always be that way. And when on those canyon trails leading to our village it was always cooler. In fact because of the small lake even with the full sun during the zenith it remained cooler than the surrounding desert.

It is here where we have our small herd, and where we grow our crops. And yes we even have a few trees, most bearing fruit of one kind or another. So we've never lacked for sustenance. While we've never had a lot, overall what we had met our needs. And in one of the side canyons we had a few mines. It was what we pulled from the ground that we traded with others. Still the traders only arrived once a year, and when it's more often, which is rare, they would only show maybe twice more.

Why is this important to know? It is because *the gift* arrived after the departure of the traders, meaning that it would be at least another year before word got out that *the gift* had manifested itself once again. And to be truthful it was much longer than that before it became known. I'd like to say that this was something exclusive to our village but that wouldn't be true. And once it arrived then many would travel to the village to seek out the one. But one of the issues lay in the fact that when the gift arrived it presented a different power to each that had received it. So in many cases once others had come to see *the one* they left disappointed because what had manifested would be of no use.

I suspect that in my sister's case it would be the same. Still, at the same time what she had is really strong . . . So strong indeed that if she touched you during one of her visions, then you'd see the same vision. And you would find yourself standing beside her inside of those images. You knew it was her, but here she appeared to be different. As I've said I felt she would be small, and when she had attained her full measure she came only to my shoulders, and I am of average height. Yet, in those visions she is tall, taller than any.

I remember the first time I became aware of her ability. Like I said she was almost four when it first happened, and to her she thought that what she did was something everybody did. And being her older brother I thought that all of it was just her imagination. Then one day she happily pointed out towards the lake and said, "Do you see them? They're beautiful!" (Beautiful was a word she was proud of, and always had carefully pronounced it.)

I looked and saw a few birds in the trees that were close to the lake and replied, "Yes, the birds are pretty."

She looked at me as if I was crazy. She put her hands on her hips in an almost perfect imitation of mother when she wasn't happy, which made me laugh. Then somewhat irritated she said, "I think they are horses."

"Horses?" I know of horses, but the only time we've ever seen any was when the traders came. And I know that she had probably seen them at that time, but we had none and could afford none. I looked really hard and only saw the birds in the trees. It was then she pointed followed by grabbing my arm.

I stood frozen because the moment she grabbed my arm the whole scene in front of me changed. We were standing on a large plain that seemed to go on forever. Catching my breath I saw, in the distance, large herds of wild horses wheeling and dancing, running and forming patterns as the colors shifted and changed. There seemed so many that it was impossible to know the size in numbers. Then she let go and the world returned to what I knew. I found I'd been holding my breath and had to let it out and begin to breathe again. I asked, "How'd you do that?" I was incredulous.

She shrugged and asked, "Do what?"

I guess to her it was a normal thing. I thought a moment, still shaken from what I had seen, and made a decision. Our sires needed to know about this. So I tentatively took her hand expecting the images to return but they were gone. I saw disappointment on her face saying to me that for her they were gone also. And so hand in hand we went back to our shelter. It was nearing the zenith meal anyway and both of them would be there.

When we entered En, seeing mom screamed a scream of happiness and ran to her wrapping her arms around her legs, looking up into mom's eyes saying, "I love you mommy!"

Smiling and looking down at her one and only

daughter mom laughed and said, "And I love you too." She looked up at me and said, "You're back early. It will be a few before the food will be on our table. So take your sister outside and wash."

I nodded and pried her off mom's legs and we went to the trough outside and cleaned up and headed back inside. At this point I didn't know how to tell them, so I waited while the five of us ate. Then I simply blurted out, "I think En has the gift."

There had been some conversation going on between my sires, and suddenly it got quiet. My, well our father, looked at me and asked, "What did you say?"

I repeated what I said, and then explained what had happened, followed by the fact that her vision had only lasted a short time. They both looked at me and then at En, and then back at me. He asked, "Are you sure? Are you sure it wasn't your imagination, or some game the two of you were playing?"

"No sir. To be honest I thought she was imagining something, but when I saw what she saw I knew better."

He turned to En and asked, "What did you see down by the lake today?"

She really hadn't been paying that much attention to what was being said as she was enjoying the food and was concentrating completely on the meal. She lifted one shoulder in a partial shrug and said, "Horses . . . lots of horses, and they were running and playing."

"And where did you see them?" He asked quietly.

As if they were there all the time she replied saying, "Oh on the other side of the water. I couldn't get to them because of that but they were having lots of fun and I really wanted to have fun with them." At that point she went back to eating. We all knew that after the meal she'd be heading for a nap.

He turned back to me with questions in his eyes. "Okay son, did you see the horses?"

"Like I said dad, all I saw was the lake, the trees and the birds, nothing more. Then she grabbed my arm and all of it vanished and I saw great herds of wild horses."

For the next few years we, as a family, tried to keep it quiet. Still we all had a chance to experience her visions, and I guess you can say that they did enrich our lives. Still, what she had been given wouldn't help any so we felt that keeping it a family secret was the best. Then one day while she had been out with her friends she came home shaken and quiet. At that very moment we knew she had experienced one of her visions and from the look on her face, and the pallor of her skin, and the fact she had tear tracks on her face told us all we needed to know.

Mom, with concern showing in every part of her being asked, "En, are you all right?"

At that moment En broke out in a fresh bout of tears and ran to mom and clung to her. This was the first of many visions that followed that shook her, and to be honest, us. Up until that first one all of her visions had been pleasant, pleasing to our minds. None of us understood, at the time, what was happening or what these visions were. And we were sure that no one would be interested in the gift that only presented images that had no real purpose or use for the world as it was.

We were all together one evening when that first different one repeated. We saw the fear in her eyes as she stared sightlessly out into nothing. To see the rest of us gathered around and held onto her. What we saw shook us to our very core. When we had come together as a family we found ourselves standing on a mountain and we saw each of us next to each other. There was a strong wind blowing and while the air was warm, the breeze was cool. We sensed more than saw that something ominous was about to take place.

I stared out into the distance and saw what had to be what we knew as a city. Cities didn't exist now, only in the past. We were too few, and the places where any might live and survive were even less. Suddenly the skies lit up with a blinding bright light right over that city, followed by a cloud of some kind climbing high into the sky. From this point of origin a large cloud layer rolled out in every direction hiding what was under it. And when we could see everything it had touched was gone.

Looking at the family and En I saw shocked disbelief. And then I, as I suspect they, realized that even here we wouldn't be able to escape that cloud of death. Panic began to rise in all of us and we desperately looked for any way to escape, but there was none. Then as this cloud began to climb the mountain approaching us at a speed greater than any horse, or anything we ever saw moving, despair and dread filled us and as one we turned to run, and then we were back in our shelter.

We looked at each other surprised that we were back, and still alive. And then we all looked at En and saw that she was shaken and crying. These images were too much for one so young. How did one deal with such? How did one stay innocent? How could one not be destroyed from such images? We reached out and held her close. It was the only thing we could do.

It was later that I began to wonder what this image was all about, what did it represent? We hadn't been there long enough to see what had actually happened to that city that was in the distance, and whether the visions she had meant anything at all. And the fact that she had no control over them, no way to suppress them meant that others like this one would arrive unbidden leaving her shaken, as well as any who happened to be in physical contact at that moment. And it was one of these incidents that finally revealed to the village that En had *the gift*. No it wasn't one of the scary ones, thankfully.

It was a few years later during one of the celebrations that included dance, song, and fellowship. During one of the dances where the entire village would dance as one, with each holding on to each other's hands, she had one of her visions. Suddenly, other than the ones playing the instruments everything went quiet. En who was in the middle with the other children, which included me of course, and all the grown ones on either side started having one of her visions, and fortunately it was one of the early ones she had many years in the past. It was of the vast herds of horses dancing and wheeling on the vast plains. And as quickly as it was there, it was gone, leaving the village breathless.

Fortunately nobody, other than the family knew

who was responsible or what such a thing represented. For now it allowed, for a short time, En to remain anonymous since the whole village experienced the vision. It became the talk of the village for a long time. Eventually, as in most things, time and other incidents put it out of the memories of most. Still such cannot remain a secret forever. And in truth, this vision seen by all had leaked out beyond, and the rumors began saying that the whole village had been given a taste of *the gift* and that there would be a great chance that someone there would be the receiver.

Well, we knew that had already happened – we the family. We all wanted to protect En, but there wasn't any way we could protect her from those visions. Visions that had to tear her apart inside as all that death and destruction came to her. Eventually, by the way she'd act and react, the ones around us began to suspect, and eventually know. We, the family knew that we wouldn't be able to keep it a secret forever. Still, in a small part of our souls we hoped to.

One day we were called to the meeting area where the leaders came together. We were confronted with what had been observed, and asked to give answers to the questions. No it wasn't put forth with suspicion or with fear. We were asked honest questions for which we knew we'd have to give honest answers. The one point we had to make, simply stated, was that *the gift* En was given would help no one. We guessed that what we saw when we were with her in those visions were images from the past. And as such would do no one in the present any good. And yes what she had was strong – strong enough that others, when in contact with En, would experience the same vision.

It didn't take long for the word to spread beyond our village, and even though it had been stated that one here in this village had *the gift* this manifestation would benefit no one. Still it didn't prevent many from making the trek from wherever they were to see and experience the gift firsthand. And it meant that somehow that our village would have to figure out how to support these additional ones putting a further strain on what we had.

Eventually the fervor died down. Since she, at this time, had no control over when these visions of hers would arrive, many would leave disappointed, and at times angry to have not experienced firsthand one of these visions. And this led to both doubt that she had *the gift* from some, and excitement from others because they had experienced and lived one of those visions. Eventually the archivists wanted to see, figuring that what she experienced might have truly been the past of this world. They wanted to write down what they saw.

In the end even they finally left. The problem, they learned, was there was no continuity, no way to tell what they saw through her visions was the past, and there was no timeline with those visions. So they had no way to know when or what happened. It was during this time that the visions became stronger, and when inside them one could use all one's senses. Now they – these visions – were as real as looking out in the morning watching the sun rise above the horizon. Real as feeling the chill of the morning, and then the warmth as the heat drove that chill away.

Now you tasted the air, felt the humidity, sensed

the subtle changes that happened when you hiked through an area. It was the smell of the greenery, the sounds of birds flying, the feel of the wind, and the moving of the grass in the grasslands as those winds created waves. And unlike before where you could only look where she was looking, one now could turn in any direction and see the whole world, and at times it would bring tears. Why tears you ask? Because what we'd see showed this world in all the beauty and variety that no longer existed. It made one want to spend all their time inside of these visions.

Yet, during all of this time, the visions covered large areas, great vistas, mountains, cities in the distance, and such – nothing up close and intimate. That would change later. Still, we appreciated what we saw. Unfortunately for her these stronger visions would wipe her out and she'd easily sleep two days before recovering. It was a worrisome thing. One so small had only so much energy to expend, and for whatever the reason, the visions seemed to require a lot.

Eventually the ones coming to see *the gift* trickled down to a few, only showing up with the traders, making it easier on everybody. And slowly as she grew she began to gain control over the visions. No, she couldn't manifest them on command, but she was able to shrink the areas down, make the scenes more intimate. And eventually we began to understand one of our yearly celebrations.

Here in this vast desert there are but two seasons, and two major celebrations. And they, the celebrations, rotate around the growing and harvesting of our crops. The first celebration has to do with the plantings and the hope for a successful wet season – such as it is – to allow our crops to grow, and the last is after the harvest where we'd gather and give thanks for the bounty. Yet, here with this celebration another seemed to be a part of it, but had no direct connection to the harvest. It was the celebration of the birth of a male child.

Now to be honest, we always feel great with the birth and survival of a child, as death seems to follow as often as life. Yet, for whatever the reason this had more significance than this. And with reverence we'd, the whole village, and as I understand it, the whole world, would honor this child. And maybe, in the end, this is why En had those visions, even though it took years for her to learn how to control them.

And we really never understood why or when this portion of the celebration had become part of us, but it had always been there, and important. We felt that what this part represented is the future, since a child coming into this world held its own promises for such. If one traveled, which I mentioned I didn't, then one would most likely see this celebration in exactly the same way everywhere, and at the same time of the year.

We, the village, were sitting around the communal fire, quietly celebrating this portion of the annual harvest celebration when I noticed En smiling, having that distant stare saying she was having one of her visions. She reached out and touched the ones on either side of her, and they realized what was happening. Shortly we were all arm in arm and enjoying what she was seeing.

So different from those of the past, as this was up

close and personal, an intimate view of this same celebration, but at the same time different. In fact it was two visions with a small break between. It explained everything to us – everything.

First we saw what might have been a desert, but in a way not really. Then we slowly got closer to what had to be a village. What and who we saw, well let's say it was different. We saw what might have been a star shining bright overhead, and in a place reserved for the animals a young woman about to give birth. And with that birth the air filled with beings that seemed to hang in the sky proclaiming the birth of this child – the very one we celebrated. To say we were in awe is an understatement.

This scene faded, and before we broke contact the second began and it was obvious that some time had passed as we were inside a room, which had to be part of someone's home or shelter. It was night, and when we looked outside it appeared to be lit up with some type of artificial light. Something we didn't have now, but we'd seen something similar in other visions of hers.

In that room was a tree, but of a type we were unfamiliar, and that tree was decorated and lit with lights of many colors. The room was warm and inviting, and there was music in the background. We heard the words, "For unto us a child is born", and we realized it had to be that child we'd seen in the previous vision. It was then as we listened in awe, that the words spoke of a Savior, and at that moment we realized that this is exactly what we celebrated now. Even after all the time from then to now, this was still with us.

Then that vision too faded away and we were back. Looking around I saw that everybody was quiet, introspective. Now we knew, now we understood. We had a rare opportunity to understand, to see, and to tie it all together. That child had come into the world to save us, to show us the light that lit the darkness. It was God providing a way to bring us back to Him.

ABOUT THE AUTHOR

F.D. Brant always wanted to write, but life got in the way. Finally after retiring he got his chance.

Storytelling and writing has always been F.D. Brant's passion, but responsibilities took preference. And because of those responsibilities it took retiring to allow those passions to come to fruition. Since retiring he has written nine books, and maintains a weekly eclectic blog, Words in the Wind.

Growing up in the backcountry he learned the appreciation of "doing things for yourself". Because it was impossible to call in someone to repair anything one either did it themselves or went without. This led to the appreciation of the natural world, and the daily struggles that one faced as nature threw problems at the family that had to be overcome, leading to confidence and self-sufficiency. This led to the strong characters that populate his stories and books. And his female protagonists are strong willed and confident – something that he saw in both in his mother and sister.